"I have a proposal."

I paused, looking back at him as the door swung partway open. My defenses came instantly up. "Please don't ruin the evening by asking me to marry you."

His grin was slow; clearly, I'd amused him. "It's not that kind of a proposal."

"That's a relief."

He eased in a little closer, planting his hand, straight-armed against the doorjamb, lowering his voice to a deeper timbre. "Let me kiss you goodnight."

The shake of my head was instantaneous.

"Hear me out," he said.

I squinted at his earnest expression, bracing myself.

"You insist there's nothing between us, no hope for a relationship."

"Because there's not."

"Then prove it. Let me kiss you goodnight and prove your point to both of us once and for all."

* * *

Husband in Name Only by Barbara Dunlop
is part of the Gambling Men series.

D0172807

Dear Reader,

Welcome to *Husband in Name Only*, book four of the Gambling Men series.

It was a delight to set another Gambling Men story in the far north—my home of several decades.

Some people know exactly what they want out of life. Adeline Cambridge knows exactly what she *doesn't* want—to fulfil her father and uncle's desire to merge the wealthy Cambridge family with the powerful Breckenridge dynasty. But Alaskan rancher turned congressman Joe Breckenridge has other ideas. He's happy to go along with a match between him and the beautiful, spirited Adeline.

He's happy to go along with a marriage, too—under any conditions she sets.

I hope you enjoy this latest story!

Barbara

BARBARA DUNLOP

———

HUSBAND IN NAME ONLY

If you purchased this book without a cover you should be aware
that this book is stolen property. It was reported as "unsold and
destroyed" to the publisher, and neither the author nor the
publisher has received any payment for this "stripped book."

HARLEQUIN®
DESIRE™

Recycling programs
for this product may
not exist in your area.

ISBN-13: 978-1-335-73548-5

Husband in Name Only

Copyright © 2022 by Barbara Dunlop

All rights reserved. No part of this book may be used or reproduced in any
manner whatsoever without written permission except in the case of brief
quotations embodied in critical articles and reviews.

This is a work of fiction. Names, characters, places and incidents
are either the product of the author's imagination or are used fictitiously.
Any resemblance to actual persons, living or dead, businesses,
companies, events or locales is entirely coincidental.

This edition published by arrangement with Harlequin Books S.A.

For questions and comments about the quality of this book,
please contact us at CustomerService@Harlequin.com.

Harlequin Enterprises ULC
22 Adelaide St. West, 41st Floor
Toronto, Ontario M5H 4E3, Canada
www.Harlequin.com

Printed in U.S.A.

New York Times and *USA TODAY* bestselling author **Barbara Dunlop** has written more than forty novels for Harlequin, including the acclaimed Chicago Sons series for Harlequin Desire. Her sexy, lighthearted stories regularly hit bestseller lists. Barbara is a three-time finalist for the Romance Writers of America's RITA® Award.

Books by Barbara Dunlop

Harlequin Desire

Chicago Sons

Sex, Lies and the CEO
Seduced by the CEO
A Bargain with the Boss
His Stolen Bride

Gambling Men

The Twin Switch
The Dating Dare
Midnight Son
Husband in Name Only

Visit her Author Profile page at Harlequin.com, or barbaradunlop.com, for more titles.

You can also find Barbara Dunlop on Facebook, along with other Harlequin Desire authors, at Facebook.com/harlequindesireauthors!

For my niece Chloe,
who's off on her own northern adventure!

One

My best friend and fellow Cal State graduate, Katie Tambour, stood on a chair in my compact dining nook, running a stud finder across the saffron-yellow wall.

"There's not much point in hanging it," I told her, not sure whether to hover up close in case she lost her footing or to stand back and mitigate the damage in the event disaster struck.

"I hung mine up this morning," she said. "I'm a pro."

My newly minted and grandly framed PhD parchment sat behind her on the small, round kitchen table. I was officially a doctor now, Adeline Emily Cambridge, doctor of philosophy, architecture and urban planning.

"You won't be moving away," I pointed out.

Katie had been offered a position here in Sacramento, lecturing on physics and astronomy at the Cal State campus. It was only part-time, but her parents lived in town, so her expenses would stay low while she built up her résumé.

"You'll be here awhile longer," she said.

"Maybe." I wasn't in any particular hurry to leave California. I'd spent the past nine years enjoying the silky air and sunshine of the state, immersed in the laid-back lifestyle and secure in my sense of freedom and self-determination.

"Found one," Katie called out in obvious delight, her fingertip marking a spot between the white kitchen cabinets and the blue and sea-green blown-glass sculpture I'd picked up at a local arts festival three years ago.

I was settled and happy in my little off-campus apartment. Only a block from the river, its balcony caught the fresh breeze on warm summer days. This far into May, my tan was golden brown from hours spent reading, researching and writing outside on my favorite lounger.

"Hand me the hammer," Katie said, reaching blindly behind herself.

"I'm not supposed to put unauthorized holes in the walls."

"It's a very small hole."

"You know I put up a damage deposit on this place."

"Nobody'll notice one more." She canted her head meaningfully toward the glass sculpture on her left. It was true that the piece had taken three hooks, and they were bigger than the ones Katie was using for my degree.

"Fine," I said on a mock huff, handing her the wood-handled claw hammer. "Go ahead, vandalize my walls."

She laughed at that, traded me the stud finder for the hammer and lined up the nail with its dangling, kinked metal hanger. "You're going to love looking up and seeing this. And you should take the credential out for a test drive—sign something *Dr. Cambridge*. I know I'll be signing everything *Dr. Tambour* for a while."

"If you do that, people will ask you for medical advice."

She tapped gently on the nail head then harder to anchor

it into the stud. "I'll tell them it's a physics degree and start explaining Planck's constant. That'll stop the questions."

"I imagine it would."

Hanger secure, she twisted around and bent over to lift the framed degree. Then she felt her way to the catch at the back of the frame, slipped it over the hanger and eyeballed the whole thing to level.

She hopped down from the chair and stood next to me. "Perfect."

I couldn't help wondering how long it would stay up there before I packed it away in a moving box.

"I got a weird job offer yesterday," I said. I'd been trying to push the unsettling letter out of my mind since it had arrived. But I knew ignoring it wasn't the answer.

"Weird how?" She stepped up and made a final adjustment to the angle of the frame.

"Surprising…concerning. I don't exactly know how to respond to it." I crossed to the kitchen counter and retrieved the crisp ivory paper from my cluttered wicker mail basket. As I handed it over to Katie, my gaze skimmed the stylistic tricolored letterhead of Windward, Alaska.

Katie folded herself into the mocha leather tub chair beside my open balcony door, next to the glass of merlot she'd abandoned twenty minutes ago, and started reading.

I could tell the second the words sank in.

"Seriously?" She looked up at me, eyes wide as the evening breeze lifted her blond hair.

"I didn't apply to it," I said. "I don't even understand how they know about me."

"You published your thesis, and the graduation ceremony was livestreamed. You're hardly a covert urban planning operative."

She read her way through the project description—to design and build an arts and culture complex for fine arts education, gallery space, retail and recreational opportunities for the third-largest city in Alaska.

I sat down on the two-cushion sofa and picked up my own glass of wine from the little coffee table between us.

It was my dream job, there was no doubt about that. And I didn't kid myself. Under normal circumstances I wouldn't get near something like it without at least ten years of experience. But there was one thing that qualified me above anyone else—I was an Alaskan.

"But..." Katie looked at me in consternation. "You said—"

"That I'd never, ever go home," I finished for her. That sentiment still held. I had no intention of going anywhere near Alaska.

"So, you'll just wait for some more offers," she said more briskly, glancing at my dining nook wall. "I mean, you're all decorated up and everything."

I could wait for more offers.

I should.

I would.

"Or you could reconsider Tucson," Katie said.

"Residential subdivisions?" I couldn't hide my grimace at the thought of doing that day in, day out.

"The salary's good, and the weather's awesome."

I plunked my head against the sofa back, closing my eyes and giving a loud snore to indicate my level of excitement about the job.

"Reno?" Katie suggested. "You'd be close enough to drive down here for the weekend."

I lifted my head. "Incorporating hotels and casinos into the community plan?" This time I gave a little shudder. "Pass."

"You better not tell me you're going to the Keys. There are snakes down there and alligators and all kinds of creepy-crawly things. I feel like you wouldn't get out alive."

"Well, there are bears in Alaska."

Katie straightened in the chair. "You're considering Alaska?"

"I just said there were bears. Does that sound like I'm considering it?"

"It's not as if the bears stroll down Main Street," Katie said.

"In Windward they do." Grizzlies could be a genuine danger all over Alaska. "Remember how you were taught stranger danger in elementary school? Well, we were taught bear aware."

Katie polished off the remaining wine in her glass and rose. "So, you prefer snakes?"

"No." Snakes scared me down to my toes. Also, alligators ate people. Bears mostly wanted people to stay out of their way. Big difference.

"Casinos aren't looking so bad now, are they?"

"I'm not excited about designing a flashy casino."

She refilled her glass at the little breakfast bar then rocked the merlot bottle my way in an obvious question.

"Please." I held up my glass. "I need to get back to them all one way or another."

I could turn down the offers and stay another month in California, hoping something better came along. Budget wasn't a problem. But I found I wanted to get going. Now that I'd defended my thesis and officially received my degree, I wanted to get started on the rest of my life.

"I find liquor is always helpful when making life-altering decisions," Katie joked as she walked my way with the bottle. "It sharpens the brain, tees up the old synapses."

I lifted my glass for her to pour. "Here's to teed-up synapses."

We said, "Cheers." And then we settled back into our seats.

"It's not going to be Reno," I said, even though I loved the idea of being within driving distance of Katie.

"Well, going to the Keys will give you perpetual nightmares, not to mention giving me perpetual nightmares worrying about you."

"And designing the Tucson suburbs would have me climbing the walls within weeks."

Katie drank thoughtfully. "You see what you just did."

I knew I'd eliminated the competition. I took a hearty drink.

"It sounds like you're going to Alaska," she said.

"My very successful father's in Alaska. My very successful uncle's in Alaska." I let out a groan of despair at the memories of growing up in the Cambridge mansion. "All of those prominent family expectations and pressures are in Alaska."

"Well…how far is it from Windward to Anchorage?"

"Not far enough."

"But there's no road, right?"

"My brothers have corporate planes."

"How will they even know you're there? Are you wearing a tracking bracelet or something? Chip in your arm?"

"My uncle Braxton will feel a disturbance in the Force."

Katie laughed.

"You laugh," I said with heavy sarcasm and a dire expression.

"Because you're funny."

"Uncle Braxton's got a wily sense of what's what and who's where."

"Your uncle Braxton's a psychic?"

I swung my glass in an arc. "My uncle Braxton's a schemer. So's my dad. And they've had their eyes on me for years as a potential asset to the family dynasty."

"You're twenty-seven years old."

"I know."

"They can't make you do anything you don't want to do."

"I know that, too." I did know that.

There was always the choice of saying no. I'd done it in the past. But that simple tactic didn't account for the guilt I'd feel when I had to turn them down for something they swore was in the best interest of the family.

I reached across the coffee table and picked up the letter again, rereading paragraph four.

Katie spoke up before I finished. "I could be your wingman—*person*…doesn't sound right that way, even though it is."

"Wingperson for what? Are we going out tonight?"

"I could come to Alaska."

I did a double take, trying to craft an amusing comeback, assuming she had to be joking.

"I'm serious," she said, looking serious. "Classes don't start up until September. I can do the course outline from anywhere."

"You're planning to run interference with my father and uncle for me?"

"Or the bears. Don't forget about the bears."

"No offense, Katie. I'd *love* to have you with me anywhere I went. You're the best friend I've ever had, but it wouldn't help. Those two are a force of nature."

"And I'm not? You can't have missed my PhD in astronomy. It's hanging on my wall now. And let me tell you, nature doesn't get anymore forceful than a supermassive black hole." She jabbed a finger in my direction for emphasis. "I've studied them. I know as much as anybody about their gravitational collapse, accretion of interstellar gas and active galactic nuclei."

"They suck the living energy out of anything that happens by, right?"

Her face scrunched up a little at my simplistic description. "At an astronomical level, yeah…basically."

"That's my dad, Xavier, and Uncle Braxton all over the place."

Katie looked confused. "I can't tell what you mean by that. Am I coming to Alaska?"

The midafternoon air was warm and clear as we stepped from the plane onto the tarmac at the Windward airport in Alaska.

"Can you smell that?" Katie asked in wonder.

"Smell what?" I detected a little jet exhaust hanging in the air but nothing noteworthy.

"Nothing! It's clear and pure, like the bubbles coming off expensive champagne. My lungs don't know what hit them."

"Champagne gives off carbon dioxide. What kind of a scientist are you?"

Katie linked her arm through mine, our backpacks tapping together. "You didn't tell me Alaska smelled so nice."

"There's no heavy industry up here." Like Katie, I inhaled deeply, reminded of the pureness of the air. "To the west, there are miles of ocean—over four thousand of them until you hit China. To the east is northern Canada—not exactly a hotbed of industrial emissions. Straight north are three national parks."

We entered the terminal building through sliding glass doors, leaving the sound of the runway behind. The decor was fresh, updated since I'd last been in the city, but the concourse was tiny compared to the international hub in Anchorage.

Katie spun around. "It's exactly what I pictured."

"That's because you searched the airport online."

"Sure, but you can't get a real feel for something until you're standing in the middle of it. This is how I thought it would feel."

People moved past us in both directions, casually dressed, most in work clothes or outdoor wear. Windward prided itself on being independent and unpretentious. Alaskans were like that in general.

As we made our way to the baggage claim—one carousel, no need to figure out where our bags would come out—I caught sight of a photo on the wall, a mural, really, since it was so big. It was clearly a dedication ceremony, maybe for the airport renovations.

Congressman Joe Breckenridge smiled knowingly down at me, and a wave of anxiety rolled through my stomach. I told myself it was just a photo. The real Joe Breckenridge was far away in DC. He spent most of his time there, the rest in Anchorage and Fairbanks, where a majority of the voters lived, or on his family ranch on the Kenai Peninsula. Still, I couldn't shake the feeling that the Alaska walls were closing in on me.

"Well, that was fast," Katie said, spotting her small suitcase and darting toward it. "Yours is here, too," she called over her shoulder.

Like the rest of the Windward passengers, I sauntered over, secure in the knowledge there was no hurry to claim my bag.

"How do we get to the hotel?" Katie asked, our bags now standing at our feet.

"It's the Redrock. They'll have a shuttle." I pointed to the ground transportation exit only steps away.

Sure enough, as the glass door slid open for us, the Redrock Hotel shuttle was waiting at the curb.

The driver approached, no suit jacket or uniform, just

a clean pair of black jeans and a gold golf shirt with the hotel logo embroidered on the pocket. "Adeline?" he asked.

"They know you?" Katie whispered in my ear with an excited lilt.

"That's me," I said to the driver. To Katie I whispered, "My name's on their reservation list."

"Hi, I'm Jackson. Welcome to Windward," the man said, shaking our hands before taking charge of our roller bags. "You want your packs up front with you?"

"Yes," I said, since my wallet and phone were inside.

"Go ahead and hop in." He took the bags to the back end of the small shuttle.

"This is great," Katie said, going for the door. "No waiting."

"You have to stop being so excited about everything," I told her.

"Are you kidding? If this was LAX, we wouldn't even be off the plane yet."

There was an older couple in the front seats of the shuttle bus. They smiled and nodded to us as we passed, heading three rows back.

"We weren't even the first ones on," Katie said, sliding her pack under the seat in front of her.

"Small means fast," I said. "Well, sometimes. Other times, remote means slow. And lots of times, *we don't have any reason to rush* means things take forever."

Katie laughed. "I like it so far."

"You've been here five minutes."

The driver entered and shut his door.

"And I'm already on my way to the hotel. Is that service or what?" She looked out the window. "I love the mountains. Look at all those trees."

"Coastal rain forest." I was feeling like a tour guide, but I didn't mind.

"There's snow up on top!"

I saw the woman in front of us turn her head to look. She was probably amused by Katie's southerner reaction.

"That's a glacier," I said. "The mountains go up over three thousand feet."

"So, it never melts."

"It never melts."

Katie sat back in her seat as the bus made its way along the coastline on Evergreen Drive. "I feel like I'm on an adventure."

"I feel like a time traveler." I thought about the photo of Joe Breckenridge back at the airport.

I couldn't help remembering the last time I'd seen him with my family in Anchorage. His brown eyes had been warm on mine, quizzical and searching, like he was trying to read me without scaring me off. Well, I had news for him. He couldn't read my mind, and I wasn't the least bit interested. Wary, sure, but only because I knew what was up.

He wasn't looking to find out if I was intelligent or funny or if we shared the same ethical and moral leanings. He'd wondered if I was like my dad and my uncle, if I could be co-opted for a common cause—the common cause of my family's business, Kodiak Communications, and Joe's political career.

Longtime friends of Joe's rancher father, my father, Xavier, and his brother, Braxton, had supported Joe's political candidacy from the start. They'd praised him to their business and social contacts, securing endorsements and propelling him to a win. After the election, he'd joined their effort to find federal money for a northern undersea cable to open the company infrastructure to European data traffic.

Afterward, they'd set their sights on me—deciding Joe

needed an Alaskan bride from a notable family, and the Cambridges needed a connection to an up-and-coming politician. It was a mutually beneficial arrangement. Too bad the bride was unwilling.

"Your family's all the way across the Gulf of Alaska," Katie told me reassuringly.

"Kodiak Communications has an installation in Windward."

"Do your brothers ever work here?"

"Rarely. And the Kodiak offices are outside town."

"There you go," she said, as if it was settled.

I believed I had a decent chance of keeping my presence a secret. If I didn't think I could pull it off, I wouldn't have considered the job. I was meeting in person with William O'Donnell, who was the director of the Arts and Culture Collective of the Chamber of Commerce, and Nigel Long, from the governor's office, first thing in the morning to finalize the details.

The shuttle bus pulled under the front awning at the Redrock Hotel, and we walked out, tipping the driver as the porter took over with our bags and led us to the front desk.

"Checking in?" the woman behind the counter asked us. Her name tag said Shannon.

"Yes," I answered. "I'm Adeline—" My gaze caught on the television screen in the lobby, showing Joe in blue jeans, a plaid flannel shirt, Western boots and a Stetson. My brain cried out, *not again*. I felt like his image was stalking me.

"Ma'am?" Shannon asked.

"Cambridge," Katie finished for me.

"I have you with us for three nights." Shannon's voice seemed a long way off as I stared at Joe Breckenridge on the flat-screen television.

It was archival footage of Joe walking through a field

with Governor Harland. The yellow-lettered chyron beneath the footage read, Meet and Greet Tonight. Congressman Breckenridge to attend a meeting at the Windward town hall.

"Are you *kidding* me?" I mustered.

"It's not three nights?"

Katie nudged me with her elbow.

I quickly shook myself back to the present.

"Leaving on the twenty-third?" Shannon asked.

"Yes. That's right." I pulled out my wallet to hand her my credit card.

"What's up?" Katie asked me in an undertone.

"Is there a hair salon in the hotel?" I asked Shannon.

"Yes, there is." She pushed a business card my way. "Through the lobby and past the elevators. It's next to the spa."

"Spa?" Katie asked with immediate interest.

Shannon smiled as she ran my credit card through the reader. "The spa hours are 7:00 a.m. to 10:00 p.m. They'll take walk-ins, but I'd advise a reservation. The hair salon hours are nine to six."

"Are you going to spruce up for the interview?" Katie asked.

"I'm thinking about it," I said.

"Is it a job interview?" Shannon asked pleasantly.

"Yes," Katie answered. Then she pointed my way. "For her."

"Well, good luck with it." Shannon handed me back my card. "I hope you'll end up staying in Windward for a good long time."

I wasn't all in on the idea yet. I was excited about the project, but the risks were starting to make themselves known. The last thing I needed was to run into Joe or have someone from Kodiak Communications recognize me.

* * *

"You look like a totally different person." Katie peered at me across the table at the upscale-rustic Steelhead Restaurant off the lobby of the Redrock Hotel. Cushioned in comfortable chairs, we were surrounded by wood accents with a beautiful light-laden mosaic of tree branches in a canopy above us. All the lighting was muted, and the windows were sparse and narrow to filter the long Alaskan daylight.

We'd ordered wild salmon citrus salads and a California chardonnay.

I wasn't convinced I loved my new hair. But I didn't hate it, either. I'd never been a blonde before, never been anything other than auburn haired.

"Bold," Katie said, leaning to one side.

I turned my head so she could have a better look and felt the short wisps at the back that no longer covered my neck. The style was parted at the side, swooped across my forehead and just a little bit spiky.

"It'll grow back if I change my mind," I reassured myself.

"Might take a while. What's with the glasses? Are you going for an intellectual flair to balance off the blond?"

Taking out my contacts was simply another way of changing up my looks. "You're blonde," I pointed out.

"I sometimes think I should go brunette, have people take me more seriously."

"People take you plenty seriously." Katie was a bona fide genius. Everyone at Cal State knew that. Hence the offer of a teaching position only minutes after she'd received her PhD.

"At Cal State, sure." She gave a dismissive laugh. "Your glasses look really cute, by the way."

They were mottled burgundy frames, slightly rounded with a tiny crystal beside the hinges.

I adjusted them on my nose, thinking it would take a while to get used to wearing them all the time. I'd used contacts consistently since I was a teenager.

"It's a decent disguise," Katie said as the waiter dropped off our wine.

"You think?" I struck a pose.

"I barely recognize you." She took a sip of her wine, and I did, too.

"Adeline?" a deep male voice intoned.

By the shiver up my spine, I knew exactly who it was.

"You're in Windward," Joe said unnecessarily, leaving his party of three other men in suits to come to our table.

I instantly regretting having cut off all that hair. "Hello, Joe."

He was dressed in a suit today, not like a cowboy. But he had the kind of frame that could pull off any style.

He looked to Katie before saying anything else, polite and friendly as always, since there was a chance she could be a voter.

"Dr. Katie Tambour, this is Congressman Joe Breckenridge."

Katie smirked at my use of her title. She nodded to him. "Congressman."

"Very nice to meet you, Katie. Do you live here in Alaska?"

And there it was.

"California," Katie answered. "Adeline and I went to school together."

Joe turned back my way. "Are you here on vacation?"

I kept my answer vague but truthful. "We're at the hotel for a couple more nights."

"Then off to Anchorage?" he guessed.

I could tell he was probing for information.

"It's not a family trip. Just me and my good friend Katie, this time."

He was clearly not satisfied, but I didn't offer anything more.

His glance back at his party, who were now seated, told me he couldn't hang around much longer.

"We won't keep you," I said.

His frown was all but imperceptible and immediately disappeared. "You're both more than welcome at the town hall tomorrow night," he said. He smoothly removed a business card from his breast pocket and set it on the table. "Or let me know if there's anything else I can do for you."

Katie lifted the card. "Thanks."

With a nod to both of us, he left for his table.

Katie leaned forward and read out loud, *"Congressman?"* as soon as Joe was out of earshot. "Look at you hobnobbing away in Alaska."

I let out a low exclamation of intense frustration.

She blinked. "What?"

"That's *him*."

"Who?"

"He's the guy."

"What guy?" Katie's brow went up, and she looked over to their table.

"Don't," I barked out.

"What?" She quickly looked back.

"I told you my dad wanted to match me up with an Alaskan."

"You did?"

"You remember—that day in the park. The café by the river. After you broke up with Andrew."

"Yeah, well, Andrew was a dud."

"I *know*. And we were talking about hometown men."

"But you said…" She paused to think about it. "Your dad picked a *specific* Alaska guy?"

I nodded.

Her gaze slid to Joe's table again.

"Don't—"

"He's not even facing this way. Your dad picked a congressman?"

I grimaced, annoyed that fate had brought Joe to town and into this restaurant tonight.

"Wow," Katie said. "Your dad aims high."

"Depends on how you look at it."

"How should I look at it?"

"He's a *politician*." I had opinions on the morals and motivations of some politicians, and Joe had never once done anything to make me believe he was any different.

"He's a tall, good-looking, successful guy," Katie countered. "And he seemed nice."

"Whose side are you on?"

"Yours. Always yours. I'm just wondering what it is you don't like about the guy."

"How about that he's open to making a deal to marry Xavier Cambridge's daughter?"

"You're exaggerating."

"I'm not."

"This isn't the 1700s."

"They're not even hiding it."

"What does he do to make you think this?"

"Okay, Joe's a little more subtle. But he's always smiling at me, friendly, trying to draw me into corners, engage in intimate little one-on-one conversations, make me laugh. And he's got these eyes, dark, espresso dark, and you can just tell he's trying to read me. He wants to know what I'm thinking, figure out how to get past my defenses and sucker me into something. Like going out on a date."

"Maybe he just likes you."

"Ha! He barely knows me."

"Okay." The skepticism was clear as day in her tone.

"I'm not imagining things. Joe Breckenridge is at the beginning of a political career. He stands a better chance of success with an Alaskan wife with deep family roots. The Cambridges want an influential politician in the family, both for soft power and to ensure a smooth regulatory framework for the expansion of the technology and tele-communications industry."

"You have it all figured out." Katie looked slightly amused.

"*They* have it all figured out. I've been hiding in California."

The waiter arrived then with our salads and sprinkled them with fresh-ground pepper.

After he left the table, Katie looked dejected.

I checked out her salad. "Your salad doesn't look good?" Mine did.

She picked up her fork. "I'm bummed you're not taking the job."

Now that the idea had sat with me for a few days, I really wanted the Alaska job. In fact, I wanted it badly enough to rationalize a reason for staying. "Joe will only be here for a couple of days."

She brightened. "And then you're in the clear."

"He does think I'm only here on vacation."

She waggled the fork. "I saw what you did with that question. Brilliantly executed."

"I didn't lie," I pointed out.

"You gently misled him."

"Yes." I gave a sharp nod, spreading my napkin in my

lap and preparing to dig into the delicious-looking salad. "No law against gently misleading."

She grinned. "He's looking at us."

I speared a slice of avocado. "Well, we're not looking at him."

Two

I met with Nigel Long and William O'Donnell at the Windward Chamber of Commerce. William's office was a former second-floor bedroom in a historical house downtown. The more I listened to William, the more excited I grew about the project.

He explained they needed someone who understood Alaskan culture. Their last urban planner was from Chicago and had been a disaster. Now they had to simultaneously secure funding, draft the plans and also engage the community to garner public support.

I was absolutely up for multitasking.

Where William was all business, Nigel from the governor's office seemed more interested in me personally—particularly my years in California and, oddly, my future plans. It was hard to get a read on him. He acted laid-back Alaskan, but his words seemed very carefully chosen.

After the meeting, we drove out to the construction site,

and I grew even more excited seeing the mountain views and the ocean so close by. I kept my enthusiasm under wraps. We hadn't finalized the details of my contract, and I didn't want to impact my negotiating position by letting them know I was dying to take this on.

The building site was far from flat. It was on a steep slope at the base of a mountain rising just north of the downtown core. I was fine with the topography. It was more interesting to design for multilevels, especially with the opportunities for ocean views.

A theater was sure to be part of the plan, and a theater didn't need any windows, so, right up front, there was a potential use for the mountain side of the site.

I craned my neck, thinking that if we went straight up a few floors, the views out front would be beyond spectacular.

"You'll be at the town hall meeting tonight?" William asked me.

I must have looked surprised by the suggestion, because he frowned then.

"Sure, of course," I quickly said. "I saw the ads after we landed."

"I'm on the panel. I probably won't say too much since the congressman's in town."

I tried not to smirk at William's acknowledgment that a congressman was sure to take up all the airtime. Politics were politics—always.

"The governor is occupied in Juneau," Nigel said. "But I'll be there to monitor and report back."

"I can formally introduce you to Joe Breckenridge," William offered.

"No," I said quickly—too quickly. The last thing I wanted was for Joe to hear that I might be staying in Windward.

"Premature?" William asked with a lift of his eyebrow.

"Yes." Agreeing with his assumption was the easiest way out.

He squared his shoulders and widened his stance. "Then let's get down to it, shall we?"

I didn't see a way or any point, really, in putting it off. "Sure."

"Does the project meet your expectations?"

It did. "Exactly as advertised," I said.

"And the site?" He looked around us. "You can see the potential."

I scanned it again myself. "I can."

"And you know what it takes to live in Alaska. I don't have to give you that spiel."

"You don't have to give me the far-north spiel." If anyone understood the challenges and advantages of living in remote Alaska, it was me.

"Any questions on your side?"

As far as I was concerned, it was down to the fine details. "Can I assume the salary will be commensurate with my education?"

He smiled at that and tossed out a very attractive number. "Plus benefits, of course, a northern living stipend and housing."

"Housing?" I was surprised by that but tried not to look it.

"The chamber owns a furnished heritage house over on Rampart Street, and we've freed it up for you. It was built in the '20s but has been updated several times since. It's the former residence of Paul Pettigrew, a fishing boat captain and one of the founders of Windward."

"He was also a bootlegger," Nigel added. "He and his bride, Rosie Jane, came from Seattle. Not that anybody believed that was her real name."

The story had me intrigued. "Why not?"

"It was rumored that she had quite a wild past before they met and married." There was a thread of judgment in Nigel's tone. "The ladies of Windward had their standards."

I found myself coming down on Rosie's side. "Sounds like she was probably just independent, given the times. I'm assuming you didn't intend to seem uptight and judgmental, right?" Actually, I wasn't too sure about that.

Nigel's pinched expression all but confirmed my thoughts.

"It was difficult on the children," William said.

That prompted another question in my mind. "Does she have descendants in town?" I wondered why the Chamber of Commerce would own the house instead of the family.

"They moved south years and years ago."

I could understand that. Who wanted to hang around a small town that had treated your mother badly?

"Back to the core question," William said. "Are you accepting the position?"

I couldn't help one more glance around the building site, thinking of a hundred ways to utilize its topography. A storied heritage house to live in for free was the icing on the cake.

I smiled and offered him my hand. "Yes. I'll take the job."

He grinned widely as we shook. "That's terrific news. Just terrific."

Nigel was a little slower on the uptake. He smiled, too, but there was something off about it. Again, I couldn't quite put my finger on his attitude.

When he spoke, there was a touch of irony in his tone. "Welcome aboard, Adeline. The governor's office looks forward to working with you."

"Thanks." I searched his expression as I shook his hand, but I didn't find any more clues.

"So, an announcement tonight?" William said.

I faltered. "Can we hold off?" I struggled to come up with a reason. "I need to talk to a few friends, family members first."

"I understand," he said. "No problem."

"I'll let you know as soon as I've settled everything on the personal side." It would be approximately the same minute Joe Breckenridge stepped on a plane out of town.

Joe was seated in the center of the panelist table on a low stage at the front of the town hall's main meeting room. The three panelists had microphones, notes and glasses of water in front of them, while an MC stood behind a podium to the right. Joe was flanked by William on his left and a fortysomething woman on his right.

Katie and I slipped in the main doors, taking chairs near the back on the left-hand end. The room was about half-full, with citizens continuing to stream inside as the clock ticked down to the start time. I had no intention of asking any questions, only gauging the perspective of the crowd about the arts and culture complex plans.

The meeting was to cover three topics—the arts and culture complex, improvements to a nearby national park, and the potential for a road linking Windward to Skagway to provide access for the panhandle city to mainland Alaska.

Katie leaned over to whisper in my ear. "He spotted you."

My gaze immediately went to Joe and, sure enough, he was looking my way.

He smiled, and I curved my lips up in return. I guessed it was too much to expect to merely blend in with the crowd.

"He's looking at you like you're made of ice cream," she said.

"Ick," I said, getting a sticky feeling.

"You're fussy for someone who hasn't had a date in six months."

"It hasn't been—" I did the math inside my head. "It's five…okay, five and a half."

"He's a really good-looking guy."

"I didn't mean ick about Joe. I mean ick about being ice cream."

Joe *was* a good-looking guy—there was no disputing that. Most women would say he was great-looking. He was tall, fit and just cowboy enough to avoid being classically handsome. He was obviously intelligent—too intelligent for his own good, I often thought. I'd sat through conversations with him and my family members—seen his eyes light up and his lips twitch with dark or irreverent humor that others didn't seem to catch.

I considered that smart, but it might have been a personal bias, since I'd caught the humor, too.

"I'd probably let him lick me," Katie said.

"Double ick!"

She laughed. "Wait, he's coming over."

"No, he wouldn't—" But I saw it was true.

He was up from his seat, had stepped off the stage and was headed our way.

"Maybe he sees someone else—" I looked behind us, hoping…

But he stopped at our row. Katie was in the end seat and he looked over her. "Curious," he said to me.

"About?" I held my breath and waited for him to elaborate, wondering what he meant and how much he knew.

He nodded to the front of the room. "Are you curious about the meeting?"

"Oh. That was a question?"

He tilted his head, looking once again like he was trying to read my mind.

"The road," I answered to throw him off. "I'm interested in the road extension."

"For Kodiak." He gave a nod of understanding.

I didn't much care if Kodiak Communications had road access to Windward or not. They'd done perfectly fine with plane and boat access up to now. But I played along.

"Will they build the road?" I asked.

"Possible. There's still the problem with the steep terrain on some sections of the coast."

I nodded to that. I did know it had been a barrier for years now. But people kept hoping the federal government would step up with enough money to shore up the hillsides and provide them with a land link out of the city.

I caught the MC's concerned look directed Joe's way, and I gestured to the stage. "I think they might be waiting for you."

Joe turned to see. "What are you doing after the meeting?"

"I'm…" A lie didn't immediately appear in my mind.

"Taking me sightseeing," Katie chimed in—great wingperson that she was.

Joe glanced at her serene expression, his jaw tightening just a little bit. "We should talk, Adeline."

"About?"

"You know what about."

"Joe—"

"Good evening, ladies and gentlemen," the MC said.

"They definitely need you up front," Katie said.

Joe gave me a look that said we weren't done talking, but then he left, striding swiftly to the stage.

"Wow." Katie blew out a breath and sat back in her chair. "That is one intense man. What do you think he wants to talk about?"

"Probably picking out names for our grandchildren."

Katie laughed.

The MC introduced the panelists.

"Have you guys ever talked about it?" Katie asked as the crowd applauded.

I joined in. "You mean sat down and said, *hey, you know how my dad wants me to marry you—what do you think of that?*"

"Yeah. Just throw it on out there."

"No." I couldn't imagine such a cringeworthy discussion.

The MC opened with a question about the national park.

"You should tell him you're not interested," Katie said.

"He knows I'm not interested. Good grief, how many broad hints does a woman have to drop?"

"Seriously? He's a guy. Some of them aren't too bright when it comes to hints."

"Joe's bright."

"You know this because?"

"I've watched him in conversations, debates, jokes."

"Jokes?"

"He gets humor." I thought back to a few specific instances with my uncle Braxton. "He's got a very dry sense of humor."

The woman sitting on stage next to Joe was talking about an interpretive center in the national park. I caught Joe's gaze on me again. It was intense, heated and almost sexy.

I silently groaned. The very last thing I needed was to start thinking Joe was sexy. I had enough on my mind at the moment.

"You should get it over with," Katie said.

"Get what over with?" I was afraid she'd guessed my sudden wayward attraction.

"Tell it to him straight. Tell him you and he are never going to happen. Tell him to find some other perfect Alaskan bride to marry."

I grinned. I couldn't help it. Joe would be stunned to silence if I was ever that direct.

"You're smiling," she said.

"It's an entertaining image."

"He's smiling back."

I focused and saw that he was. I was instantly sucked into the invitation of his open expression. I shouldn't react this way. He might be sexy, but I wasn't going to be swayed.

I quickly sobered, and his expression turned cajoling.

I realized we were having a conversation across the crowded room.

"It might work," Katie said.

"He'd only take it as a challenge." That was my fear.

Joe could tell I didn't want to pursue a relationship, but it hadn't deterred him for one moment.

"Do you have a better idea?" she asked.

"Stay out of Alaska." I knew I hadn't taken my own advice.

The MC invited Joe to speak, and he leaned slightly toward the microphone, his deep voice resonating through the hall, stilling the crowd. It was easy to see how he got people to listen to him. People should listen to him—about his ideas, at least. But not me. And not about whether or not to date him.

"Adeline?" Kate asked.

"Hmm?"

"You sure it's not something else?"

I turned to her. "What else?"

"Are you afraid you might be attracted to him?"

"No." My answer was instantaneous even as I felt a hot little rush go through me.

"Uh-oh," Katie said.

"There's no uh-oh."

"Oh, *you're* not attracted to him, not one tiny little bit."

I wanted to flat-out lie again, but I didn't lie to Katie. "He's physically attractive. You said it yourself. He's physically attractive, but that's all. That's it. Most of the time he annoys me."

She considered me for a moment but seemed to accept my answer. "Okay."

"Good." I felt like it was settled.

"You should tell him, though."

"He'll be gone by tomorrow." And my troubles would be over—at least temporarily.

Katie seemed to consider. "I suppose avoidance is another approach."

"It's worked for me so far." I tuned into Joe speaking about the potential road access. He was eloquent, empathetic and enthusiastic.

"He's got a nice voice," Katie noted in an undertone.

It was true. The audience was riveted to his words, nodding and smiling, bursting into applause after he finished speaking even though he hadn't promised any action.

The MC then asked him about the arts and culture complex.

He gave almost the same answer, and, again, no one seemed much bothered by its vagueness. They listened carefully, nodded to each other, laughed when he made little jokes and applauded at the end as if he'd said something astounding.

"How does he do that?" I asked Katie beneath the cover of the applause. "I mean, okay, he's got the gift of gab, but they're eating right out of his hand. He could recite a plumbing manual and they'd clap."

Katie chuckled at my joke. "That's obviously how he got himself elected. He's giving them what they want."

"But what does he stand for?"

"Happy voters."

"That's what's so frustrating."

"About Joe Breckenridge?"

"About politics. I hate all the wishy-washy. Take a stand already."

Joe was now listening politely to William's outline of the arts complex project status. He nodded in spots then led the applause at the end, saying what looked like congratulatory words to William.

If I had to guess, I'd say the crowd was equally split between those excited about the arts and culture complex and those excited about the road extension. The national park improvements were a smaller project, the next phase of ongoing longer-term upgrading, so it didn't garner the same level of interest.

For me, it was satisfying to see so many in the community were supportive of the arts and culture project. I couldn't wait to get started on the community engagement.

Katie and I made a clean getaway from the town hall meeting, and Joe left Windward the next morning. I knew that because they covered his departure on the local news. Katie then offered to fly back to Sacramento and orchestrate my apartment move so I could start the job right away.

She was still determined to live with me in Alaska for a couple of months until her teaching job started, seeing it as an adventure vacation for herself. I was more than happy to have her company. The Captain Pettigrew house was plenty big enough for both of us.

A rabbit warren of small rooms and twisting corridors, the old house featured gleaming hardwood floors and walls, ornate period furniture, a massive dining table, and a china hutch full of wonderful pieces of Wedgwood in a turquoise-and-russet pattern. The living room held a pair of massive French Provincial armchairs, taupe with a golden luster on the wood accents. They had cloud-soft cushions and deeply tufted backs. They sat across from a satin burgundy sofa accented with gold stitching and tiny fleurs-de-lis.

The side tables, the stained glass lamps and a grandfather clock were meticulously reproduced and restored. Luxurious emerald drapes framed the paned windows, held back by thick ropes that added to the opulence.

The house had four bedrooms in all, one on the main floor set up as an office. I took the master that was also on the main floor, thinking it would be most convenient for the long term. Katie picked one of the sloped-ceiling second-floor bedrooms with a queen-size bed, a little reading nook and three dormer windows. Thankfully, the bathrooms had been remodeled recently. And the kitchen was a perfect combination of period look and modern convenience, with white-painted cabinets, long butcher-block countertops and a faux woodstove that ran on propane gas.

Four days in, with a hundred nooks and crannies left to explore, I still couldn't believe I had the chance to live here.

I didn't have a car yet. I'd decided against moving my five-year-old compact from California. It would be easier to buy something here in town. Plus, I'd need four-wheel drive once winter arrived and the roads turned snowy and slippery. While maneuverability was important in Sacramento, with crowded traffic and tight parking stalls, stability counted around here. In Alaska, roads were wide, parking was generous and pickup trucks were the most popular mode of transportation.

My house was less than a mile from the Chamber of Commerce offices, so I'd taken to walking to and from work. My temporary office cubicle was a hived-off space at the top of the staircase beside the Chamber of Commerce. William told me I was also welcome to work from home until the temporary field office was set up with construction trailers out on the building site. But that would be several weeks down the road.

For now, although I loved the little office in Pettigrew House, I also liked working around the people in the Chamber of Commerce building.

"Morning, Adeline," receptionist Stella Atwater called out as I entered the main floor. Thirty-three, dark haired, dark eyed, stout and very fit, she was the backbone of the Chamber, knowing everyone and everything that happened around Windward.

"Morning," I replied as her little beagle, Snuffy, peeked out from under her desk then trotted over to meet me, tail wagging. "And good morning to you, Snuffy." I bent to give him a scratch on the head.

"William is looking for you," Stella said.

"Did he try to call?" I reached into my bag for my phone, thinking I must have missed the ring, maybe while I was passing the Starfish Restaurant renovation site a few blocks back. They'd been jackhammering the patio concrete.

Stella shrugged. "He just asked me to send you up to his office. It didn't sound urgent or anything. He's not upset."

I'd have been surprised if he was upset. William was easy to get along with, focused on his work but incredibly even-keeled. I was guessing it would take a lot to upset him.

I headed straight up the stairs, dropping my bag in my cubicle and tucking my phone into the back pocket of my gray slacks, then pushing up the sleeves of my speckled gray-and-white pullover.

William's office was down a short hallway, past the little unisex bathroom and around a corner to the back of the building.

I knocked on his partly open door.

"Yes?" came the reply.

I opened the door.

He waved me in with a smile, his phone at his ear. "Certainly. She's here right now."

I slipped into the guest chair across his desk to wait.

"And we appreciate the opportunity," he said. "The Forberg." He made a note on a scratch pad, hung up the phone and gazed at me for a moment.

"Morning," I said into the silence, attempting to gauge his expression.

Stella was right. He didn't seem upset. He seemed... curious.

"Good morning," he said back.

I didn't want to be nosy, so I didn't ask about the call, waiting to see if he'd share.

Instead, he stood up and rounded to the back of his chair, leaning the heels of his palms against it. "That was Congressman Breckenridge's office."

I stilled, going on alert.

"The congressman wants to discuss additional funding options for the project."

"That's a good thing," I ventured, thinking funding was always a good thing.

"With you."

Well, that part wasn't good. "Why me? Wait, how does he know I'm on the project?"

William drew back. "I don't know. Why wouldn't he know you were on the project?"

"We didn't announce it. And then he left town."

"I don't think he left the planet. It's been mentioned on a few news websites now, and it's been in the paper, of course."

I realized my reaction had sounded inane. "Sure. No

problem. Just the three of us?" I assumed William would be on the call.

"Just the two of you."

It took a second for William's words to sink in. "You know more about the project than I do. He's interested in getting to know our team."

"You're the head of the team."

"He already knows me," William said.

I almost spoke up to say the Congressman knew me too…almost.

"Before he goes to bat for us, he wants to assure himself we can execute the project."

"We can," I said, annoyed with Joe for inferring that I couldn't manage a commercial construction project. What did he think I'd been learning all these years? Both my master's and my PhD studies had included practicums and internships. I knew what I was doing.

"This is an opportunity, Adeline. We're not fully funded yet, and we need a significant federal commitment before we break ground."

I steadied my emotions. I was a professional, and this was part of the job. "Of course. I understand completely. Did his office set a time for the call?"

"No need."

I blew out a breath of relief. If they hadn't set up the call yet, other priorities might come up, and there was a chance it wouldn't happen.

"He's on his way back to Alaska."

"No."

William looked baffled by my reaction. "What do you mean, no?"

"I mean… I'm surprised. He just left. I thought he went back to DC." I hesitated. "That's what was reported."

"Well, I suppose his schedule changed." William peeled

off a yellow note from on top of his desk and held it out to me. "The Forberg Club, five thirty."

"Tonight?" I didn't even get a day or two to get used to the idea?

"Tonight. He'll have booked a meeting room. So just check with the front desk. Have you been there before?"

"No."

"Really? Kodiak Communications has a membership."

"I don't work for Kodiak."

"Right. It's on Peel Road, just off Evergreen toward the water. There's a private elevator from the lobby to the third floor."

I came to my feet and took the little slip of paper. "I'll find it."

A few choice words echoed through my brain as I walked back to my desk.

"Game," I said out loud as I put my phone down on the desk and plunked into my chair. "Set and match. Well played, Congressman." I closed my eyes for a brief second and gave my head a shake.

Then I squared my shoulders and powered up my workstation. This was a professional meeting, not a personal one. I would have every available fact, figure and talking point committed to memory before I got anywhere near the Forberg Club.

Joe wanted to talk arts and culture complex? Fine. We'd talk arts and culture center and absolutely nothing else.

The Forberg Club was the closest Windward came to a five-star establishment. Since I'd packed mostly Alaska casual, I dressed up the single dress I'd brought as much as I could. It was basic black, with a snug, sleeveless bodice and a lightweight A-line skirt that fell to midthigh. I topped it with a cropped, lightweight burgundy sweater for color. I'd brought a pair of heeled black ankle boots that were workable. Then I added a platinum starfish necklace that twinkled with little diamond chips along with my favorite diamond stud earrings my brother Mason had given me for my twenty-first birthday.

Since the jig was up anyway, I wore my contacts and moussed the waves out of my newly blond hair so it flowed smoothly across my forehead, hanging partway down my cheek on the right side. The style and color took a bit of getting used to, but I'd decided it was at least fresh and fun.

I'd expected to be shown to a meeting room at the Forberg, but the hostess took me on a circuitous route through the well-spaced, polished wood tables and round-back leather chairs of the dining room.

Joe rose from a corner table in a crisp white shirt, a silver tie and a perfectly cut suit.

"Adeline." He smiled, coming around to pull out my chair as the hostess took her cue and left us alone.

I gave him a disapproving look. "This isn't a date."

"I know. It's a meeting." He gestured to my chair.

"We're in a restaurant."

"We're in a business club."

I deepened my frown.

"I'm starving," he said. "I had a tight connection in Anchorage."

"They didn't serve a meal in first class?"

"Somewhere over Montana, but that was hours ago. Sit down."

I hesitated a second longer, though I wondered why I was being so obstinate. It was probably better that we were meeting in public anyway. "You know I'm expected to ask you for money."

"We don't have to talk about that right now. Sit down, relax." His low tone was right in my ear.

"That's asking a lot." But I sat down.

"You won't be sorry," he said as he returned to his own seat. "They serve great steaks, seafood—whatever you're in the mood for."

"Our first community engagement event will be next week." I started right in on my rehearsed spiel. "And we're framing up other engagement tools such as a feedback form and a survey for the website. The website launch will coincide with—"

"Would you care for a drink?" he asked.

Out of the corner of my eye, I saw the waiter coming up on our table. I stopped talking.

"A glass of wine?" Joe asked me. "A martini? Old Fashioned?"

"Wine is fine," I said. The last thing I cared about was what I had to drink. "Whatever you're having."

My answer seemed to surprise him. But he quickly rolled with it. "Do you have a bottle of Château Cinq Rivières 2003?"

"I expect we do," the waiter answered. "If not, is the 2005 acceptable?"

"Yes. That would be fine."

"I'll be right back." The waiter left the table.

"As I was saying, the website launch will coincide—"

"Adeline."

"—with the first public meeting, so that the marketing efforts for—"

"Are you going to do this all night?"

"Talk about the arts and culture complex? Yes, I am." He fought a grin.

"Don't you dare act like I'm delightful. I'm not being delightful."

"You are delightful."

I stifled an exclamation. "You *see* why you make me so frazzled?"

"No, I don't. I don't see how I can possibly make you frazzled. You barely even know me."

"I know enough."

The waiter came back with a bottle of red wine, cradled in a white linen napkin so Joe could read the label. "Cabernet sauvignon Château Cinq Rivières 2003."

"Perfect," Joe said.

The waiter produced a corkscrew and extracted the cork, carefully pouring a measure into Joe's glass.

Joe swirled it around for a minute to aerate it before taking a sip.

"That's fine," he said to the waiter, who then poured my glass before topping up Joe's.

"As I was saying," Joe continued as the waiter walked away. "You don't know me at all."

"I've known you for years."

"You practically run out of the room every time I show my face."

"I sat next to you at dinner last August."

I escaped his wry smile by taking a sip of the wine. The wine was fantastic—off-the-charts fantastic. Okay, so maybe there was an upside to this meeting, after all.

"One hundred points?" I asked, setting down my glass.

"Don't change the subject."

"This is a fantastic wine."

"That's why I ordered it. You barely spoke to me last August."

"There were eight of us at the table."

"And you talked to the other six."

"Mostly to Sophie. She was new to the family then." My long-lost cousin, Sophie, had met us for the first time only weeks before that dinner. I'd felt obligated to ensure she felt welcomed into the family.

"Why are you deflecting?" His blunt question gave me pause.

I looked straight into his eyes for the first time since I'd arrived. I was thinking maybe Katie was right and it was time to be honest. "Reflex, I think."

"Now, *that* was honest." He lifted his glass.

I followed suit and took another sip. "Do you blame me for rebelling?"

"Against your father and Braxton? No. Against me? Yes."

"I don't see how I do one without the other. I feel like a bride from some noble family in the Middle Ages, bartered for a suitable match, an advantageous alliance, a dowry, the whole bit."

"Have I ever once proposed?" His question was delivered so seriously but was so ludicrous that I had to stifle a laugh.

"And for the record," he continued in the same vein, "nobody ever offered me a dowry."

I shook my head, fighting off the grin.

He smiled serenely. "But you are a valuable little treasure. A few hundred years ago, your family could have done well," he teased.

I all but growled at that.

He ignored me. "Spirited. Beautiful. At least you were before you cut off all your hair."

I self-consciously touched the short wisps of hair beside my ear.

"I'm joking," he said. Then he lowered his voice and leaned slightly forward. "I'm sorry. That was rude. You're still beautiful, though I did love the color it was before. Why did you change it?"

I had no intention of telling him the truth on that count.

I adopted a breezy tone, lifting my wineglass as I spoke. "Something fresh for the summer. A celebration of graduation."

"Congratulations on that, by the way... Dr. Cambridge."

"I don't plan on using the title." I took another sip.

"Up to you, of course. Although I'd enjoy seeing you make your brothers use it when they address you."

I couldn't stop a smile at the thought of my brothers' reaction to that.

I quickly smoothed out my expression. I didn't want to have fun tonight. "Say, did you ever meet the Chicago guy?" I jumped on my first idea to change the subject.

"What Chicago guy?"

"My predecessor on this project."

A blank look on his face, Joe shook his head.

The answer confirmed my suspicions about the purpose of this dinner. "We're not here to talk about arts center funding."

"We can talk about arts center funding."

My expression called him out for lying. "But that's not why we're here."

He swirled the wine in his glass again and took another drink. "Let's get that out of the way. What do you need?"

William had given me very specific instructions for a deliverable. The federal government had announced the Rural Expansion Fund, a special pot of money for lower-population states to improve their infrastructure. Competition was going to be tough, but Windward had a good chance of getting approval for one project—either the arts and culture complex or the road expansion.

"We need your pledge to support the arts and culture complex on the official state application to the federal Rural Expansion Fund."

"Done. It's a worthwhile project that the whole com-

munity can benefit from, and I'm sure you'll do a pow-
erhouse job executing the build. Tell William you had to
work really hard to talk me into it." He lifted the bottle
and topped up each of our glasses. "Now can we relax and
enjoy dinner?"

I decided to take yes for an answer, and we settled into
king crab salads and fresh halibut with wild mushroom
risotto.

Joe dropped the subject of my family and the two of us
while I let the funding and project discussion end. Instead,
we compared thoughts on a just-released feature film that
had been set in Juneau, moving on to other movies, then
books, disagreeing on some but finding common ground on
others. We both liked biographies and classic spy thrillers,
especially Hitchcock and Orson Welles.

Near the end of the meal, I caught sight of Nigel Long
two tables over. I might not have noticed him except that
he was looking quite intently our way.

I smiled to be polite, and he smiled back, but his features didn't line up. His lips curved, but his eyes stayed
sober, leaving me with the now-familiar unsettled feeling.

"What is it?" Joe asked as I turned my attention to the
dessert menu in the middle of our table.

"Nigel Long," I said.

"I saw him come in."

"I get the feeling he doesn't like me."

Joe glanced over. "It's me he doesn't like."

"Why not?"

"Governor Harland is not my biggest fan."

"Why?" I opened the slim dessert menu, more as a dis-
traction from Nigel's gaze than because I was still hungry.

"The governor wants the access road, not the arts and
culture center. I wouldn't commit to backing him."

"Nigel told me the governor was supportive of the arts complex."

Joe gave a grim smile. "He would."

"Sneaky. I haven't really warmed up to the guy."

"He's always polite to me. But he's the kind of guy who interacts solely with power, money and titles."

Coming from a family with means, I understood what Joe meant. "You must get that all the time."

Joe nodded. "It's frustrating, never knowing if people actually like you or think you're smart or funny."

"You're smart and funny." I was honest before I thought to censor myself. I decided it must be the wine.

"People nod at my wisdom and laugh at my jokes even when they're secretly thinking I'm wrongheaded and boring."

"Because you control the purse strings."

"I influence them."

I felt a little guilty then. "You do know that's why I'm here."

"I know exactly why you're here, Adeline."

"Do you hate me for it?"

"I admire you for it."

I was confused by the answer, since I was one of the people using him for money. "Why?"

"Because you manned up, or womanned up, and put your responsibilities ahead of everything else and came on out here for the good of your project, even though it was the last thing you wanted to do. Let's treat ourselves to some dessert."

I expected him to open his menu, but he rose from the table instead and straightened his jacket.

"What are you doing?"

"No need to hang around the Nigel Longs of the world," Joe said with a sidelong glance at the man. "I know a better place."

Three

We made our way down the shore to a bustling restaurant called the Pirate Pies. It was a funky little open-air place overlooking a rocky beach with waves and salt spray billowing up nearby. The breeze was brisk, but high plastic barriers sheltered the diners. The Plexiglas was scuffed and scratched, slightly obscuring the view of the late-night setting sun.

Joe shucked his jacket, and we climbed onto side-by-side bar-height chairs at the end of a long, narrow table where three other parties were already seated spaced along its length.

"This doesn't seem like you," I said as I got settled on the worn paint of the wooden chair. Mine was blue, or used to be blue, where Joe's used to be yellow.

He glanced around. "In what way? The delicious pies or the fantastic view?"

"You know what I mean. It's not stuffy."

"Who says I'm stuffy?"

"You've always been stuffy around me."

"Not when I'm on the ranch."

"Been on the ranch much lately?" I asked with an arch of my brow.

"I rode at your dad's place in August."

It was true. Joe usually rode horses with one or both of my brothers when he visited our family. The Cambridge horse stable was a sideline left over from my great-grandfather. Our home was on rare Alaskan agricultural land, and we still ran horses on the lush grasses, leasing the horses out to an eco-tourism outfit in the summer season.

"Hey, Joe," a man called from down the table.

"Evening, Ben," Joe responded with a nod.

"Have you met my wife, Petra?" The man motioned to the woman at his side. "We liked what you had to say about the park at the town meeting."

"Glad to hear it," Joe answered. "Nice to see you, Petra."

I could see a few other people glancing Joe's way.

"Are the wheelchair-accessibility trail upgrades going through this year?" another woman asked.

"Definitely," Joe told her. "They'll be fully accessible all the way to hot springs."

"That's good." The woman nodded. "My mom hasn't been up there in years, and she'd love to go back."

"Is your mom Jane Mitchell?"

"That's her."

"Tell her I say hi, and I'll keep her posted on the progress."

"Thanks, Joe," the woman said, looking pleased.

"Joe this, Joe that?" I whispered to him, surprised by his laid-back manner. "Not Congressman Breckenridge?"

"They're good people," he said back in an undertone.

"They've had my back, and now I've got theirs." Louder, he said to me, "I'd try the key lime if I was you."

Someone else chimed in, "The pecan's to die for."

"I'm having bumbleberry," a new voice added.

"If you get the apple, definitely go with *both* the cheese and the ice cream."

I gave appreciative smiles and nods to all of those making suggestions before turning to Joe. "And what are you having?"

"Key lime," he said, looking surprised by my question. "Would I steer you wrong?"

We both had key lime, and it was as to die for as any pie I'd ever tasted. Afterward, Joe walked me home, insisting on it even though it was only a few blocks more, and it was barely twilight. This close to the summer solstice, the sky stayed blue all night long.

"William must really want you to stay," Joe observed as we walked up the scuffed concrete sidewalk to the Pettigrew house porch.

"I'd have stayed without the house," I said as we passed through the row of white pillars on the porch.

I was feeling unusually relaxed around Joe—maybe it was his manner with the people at the Pirate Pies, or maybe it was the reminder of his ranching roots. But, in the moment, taking Katie's advice seemed like the most practical path forward.

I turned to face him at the door, deciding to be up front and honest about where I was going in life and his role in it. "This project is a fantastic opportunity for my career."

"I'm glad to hear that."

"I really want it to work out. I want it to go smoothly and simply."

"Seems like it probably will."

"I have plans for my future," I continued. "I hope you

can understand that. I don't want pressure from my dad and Braxton to interfere."

"I understand," he said with a nod.

"That includes you." I wanted to be crystal clear.

He gave a ghost of a smile. "I know what you're saying."

I turned and inserted the key and turned the cut-glass doorknob. "Thank you."

"But I have a proposal."

I paused, looking back at him as the door swung partway open. My defenses came instantly up. "Please don't ruin the evening by asking me to marry you."

His grin was slow; clearly, I'd amused him. "It's not that kind of a proposal."

"That's a relief."

He eased in a little closer, planting his hand, straight-armed against the doorjamb, lowering his voice to a deeper timbre. "Let me kiss you good night."

The shake of my head was instantaneous.

"Hear me out," he said.

I squinted at his earnest expression, bracing myself.

"You insist there's nothing between us, no hope for a relationship."

"Because there's not."

"Then prove it. Let me kiss you good night and prove your point to both of us once and for all."

I wasn't buying it. It couldn't be that simple. "Are you promising to drop the idea?"

"I haven't exactly been promoting it up to now."

That was fair. He hadn't.

I admitted it. "You've been…persistent…patient."

"Patient is a bad thing?"

"You're always just—"

"Waiting." His voice was a rumble as he bent his elbow

and eased closer still. "I'm waiting for you to give me a chance."

"There is no chance, Joe. My family can't simply *will* us into being a thing. Life doesn't work that way."

"Okay. But back to my proposal." He waited. His dark eyes once again seemed to be searching my soul.

"Okay. I'll do it. But only if you promise, if you *promise* to stop hovering on the periphery of my life."

"Yeah?" He looked happy.

"You heard the whole thing, right?"

"I heard."

"Well, then…" I took a bracing breath, tipped my chin and tilted my lips.

"Don't look like you're going to the gallows."

He almost made me smile with that. I did feel a little like a condemned woman. "At least you gave me a last meal."

His palm came up to frame my cheek. "Plus dessert." He bent his head, moving in closer. His breath puffed softly against my face.

I steeled myself.

"Adeline."

"What?"

It was a beat before he answered. "Never mind." His free arm gently circled my waist while his fingers sifted into my hair, cupping the base of my neck as his lips brushed mine.

The first touch was light but somehow electric. Little pulses of energy sent a warmth through my chest and left me shocked to stillness.

He kissed me again, more firmly this time, his lips engulfing mine with such surprising tenderness that I kissed him back. It caught me off-guard.

I felt like I couldn't trust myself. His forearm tightened across the base of my spine, and I molded against him, feeling his body heat teasing me from my shoulders to my knees.

He deepened the kiss, and I opened to him, feeling a surge of emotions propel me further. My arms wound around his neck, and I clung there, tipping my head back, accepting kiss after kiss.

I was vaguely aware of him pushing open the door and kicking it shut, then backing me into the front hall. I was more aware of his hands moving down my backside, along my thighs, coming to the hem of the little black dress.

I gasped for air, filling my lungs, giving myself more energy to kiss him harder, explore the contours of his shoulders, push the frustrating barrier of his suit jacket out of the way, not caring that it crumpled to the floor. His cotton shirt was thin, and I could feel the ripple of his taut muscles, their smooth roll to his biceps that felt strong and sexy. Powerful.

I leaned into his chest and kissed him through the white cotton, dampening the fabric.

He gave a low moan, and his hand swooped up the inside of my bare thigh, under the filmy skirt to the silky panties that were no barrier at all.

His lips were back on my mouth, his tongue tangling with mine. His hand cupped my breast, and my nipple tightened, sending shards of arousal to my very core.

It was my turn to moan.

His shirt was a barrier now, and I pulled the buttons free, running my hands over his smooth chest, kissing his skin, tasting the salt.

He shucked his shirt and then pushed down the strap of my dress, kissing my bare shoulder. He kissed his way across my chest, between my breasts, baring more cleavage as he went.

I tipped my head back, offering my neck, my lips and everything else.

He scooped me into his arms, kissing my mouth as he crossed the room.

In seconds we were in my bedroom.

He lowered me to the bed and stripped off my panties, tossing them away. It had only been seconds since his mouth had been on mine, but I missed his lips already.

Then he joined me there, kissing me over and over. I tugged at my dress, and he pushed it out of the way before getting rid of his pants.

I wrapped my legs around his glorious nakedness. He tried to speak, but I was beyond listening. I kissed him hard and deep, arching against him, pulling him into me, telling him yes and whispering his name on harsh gulps of air.

He held me tight, increased his rhythm, kissed my lips, my face, my neck and my breasts. Desire spiraled in a hot, tight core, blocking out the room, the house, the world as pleasure pulsed faster and faster between us until it sang like a starburst, engulfing me in glorious relief.

The first thing that came back was Joe's breath in my ear, then his heartbeat against my chest, then his slick skin and his slightly trembling fingertips feathering along the curve of my hip.

I knew what I'd done. And I knew why I'd done it. I hoped he understood.

"I think *that* proves my point," I said in a choppy, breathless voice.

"Sure," he answered, his chest rising as he inhaled. "No attraction there, nothing to build on."

I was glad we were on the same page. "Exactly."

He eased his weight from me, moving to his side. "It's too bad, though."

"Why?" I didn't think it was too bad at all. Now we could both get on with our lives.

"Because that was some mind-blowing sex we just had."

"*Sex* being the operative word."

"Okay." He sounded half confused, half amused.

I turned my head his way, pulling back just enough to focus and reinforce my point. "If this was romantic, you'd have bought me flowers, read me poetry—"

"Poetry?"

"—discovered my likes and dislikes and eased your way into gentle, respectful lovemaking."

"Poetry?"

"This was a hormone-fueled, chemistry-laden, instinctive scratch-an-itch kind of thing. It had nothing to do with romance or genuine attraction." I paused for a breath, because I was still pretty winded. "I don't know about you, but it's been a while for me."

"You're saying this was nothing but pent-up sexual energy?"

I gave him a smile and an approving pat on the shoulder. Once I touched him, I wanted to keep my hand right there, but I forced myself to pull it away.

"That's one way to look at it." He turned so he was staring at the ceiling.

"So." I made my tone brisk and no-nonsense. "I assume you're heading back to DC now and I can carry on here?"

"That was my plan."

"Good. You'll still support our financial aspirations?" I wanted to be able to report back to William tomorrow that the meeting had been successful.

The back of Joe's hand still touched mine, and he lifted them together. "I'll support you, Adeline."

I gazed at our joined hands for a moment, marveling

at the differences. His was large and rugged, the fingers long, his skin thicker and slightly callused.

"Can we keep this all quiet?" I asked. "I mean, my family—"

"I won't say anything to your family." He sounded affronted.

"Thanks, Joe."

He unexpectedly kissed my hand. "You're welcome, Adeline. This is not how I expected our meeting to end."

"Me, neither. But I'm relieved we got everything settled."

William was beyond pleased that Joe had given us his support. Alaska's Senator Rachel Scanlon was a wild card; nobody knew which of the two projects she'd support. Governor Aaron Harland claimed to be neutral, but we now knew he wanted the access road.

I was more than relieved to have my family's matchmaking nonsense put to rest between me and Joe. I felt like a huge weight had been lifted from my shoulders. Joe had also promised to keep quiet about me being in Alaska, so I wouldn't have to worry about my father and uncle interfering, either.

The arts and culture center's first two community engagement meetings attracted a range of arts and community groups, along with many other Windward citizens. The meetings went well, and with Joe's support on the financial front, the on-site office was being set up for the initial planning work so we could apply for the rest of the funding.

I was busy putting the broad strokes of the community recommendations into a coherent report and helping William set up contracts with architectural, engineering and construction companies. The mayor had even sent us an encouraging email, asking to be involved and offering assistance from the city of Windward.

Since I didn't need any furniture for the Pettigrew house, Katie had put most of my things in storage, arriving with boxes full of our personal items. I was most excited to get my full computer station up and running, but I was also thrilled to be able to expand my wardrobe.

In the home office, she and I pushed a two-cushion sofa off to one side, parking it in front of a built-in bookcase. Then we decided one of the lamps had to go to give me enough room for a proper workstation. Luckily, the antique desk was huge, and a side table could be pulled around to set up my biggest monitor.

It became obvious that the house was built in an era when few electrical outlets were needed. But a power strip solved that problem, and we held our breath as we got ready to power everything up at once. We hoped the load wouldn't trip the breaker—like it had in the kitchen when we ran the microwave, the blender and the coffee maker all at the same time.

"You don't dare bring a coffee maker in here," Katie said, unplugging two of the lamps on the far side of the room to lessen the load.

I'd decided I could make do with the overhead light. "And…contact." I pressed the button for the last of my three monitors.

We both looked around the room.

"Hold real still," Katie said.

"I think it's going to work," I said.

"We have achieved electricity!"

I clicked an icon with my mouse and watched the architectural software package fill the screens. "Better than that. We've achieved technology." I could now put my notes and drawings into the proper tool.

"This calls for a celebration."

It was Friday afternoon. So, in just a couple of hours, I'd be officially off duty until the next public meeting on Sunday afternoon.

"We need cake," Katie said.

"We could walk down to the grocery store," I suggested. "The bakery's almost two miles away." I didn't mind the walk, but that was a long way to carry a cake home, especially in the warm sunshine.

"I meant make our own. I've been dying to take that oven out for a test drive. Besides, now that we've unpacked, I feel like nesting."

"You want to bake a cake?"

I was definitely not the most domesticated person in the world. I'd grown up with chefs doing the cooking at our house in Anchorage, and there were great takeout restaurants in Sacramento. There'd been little need for me to cook for myself, never mind bake. The closest I came was toasting my own bagel and spreading it with cream cheese.

"Baking is fun," Katie said. "You've got some ripe bananas in the kitchen. It'll be almost healthy."

"Banana cake?"

"With cream cheese frosting."

I wasn't about to say no. "You'll have to tell me what to do."

"Easy-peasy." She started for the kitchen. "We'll need a mixing bowl and a couple of pans."

We had fun hunting through the kitchen cupboards, finding everything from cheese graters and corkscrews to the baking pans and ceramic mixing bowls we needed for our cake.

Katie found instructions for the oven and got it heating. Then she set me up mashing the bananas while she mixed butter and sugar.

"I took your advice," I said. I'd been waiting to talk to her in person about Joe.

"You're mashing them really smooth?"

"Mashing?"

"The bananas."

"Oh, sure, that, too."

"What else?" She'd found an electric mixer for the butter and sugar, and the whirr of the motor filled the air.

I waited until she was done and scraping down the sides before I spoke. "With Joe."

She stopped what she was doing and turned to look at me. "What Joe?"

"He came back again."

"Here? To Windward?"

"Yes."

"When?"

"A few days after you left. Turns out the funding push gets complicated." I continued my banana-mashing efforts. "There's competition between the arts and culture complex and the road extension."

Katie was still staring at me. "And the Joe part?"

"William wanted Joe's support to push the project in DC, and Joe said he wanted to get to know the team to decide if we could execute the project."

"Team? What team?"

"Exactly," I said, glad Katie caught on right away. "*I'm* the team. So, we met at the Forberg Club."

"What's that?"

"Very high-end, very snooty, private mover-and-shaker kind of place down on Peel Road near the water."

"You, Joe and William?"

"Me and Joe."

"Just the two of you?" Katie looked intrigued now.

"Yes. It was the perfect opportunity. So, I did what you said."

Katie smiled with obvious satisfaction as she crossed to the fridge and pulled out the egg carton.

"I threw it all out there," I continued. "I told him in no uncertain terms that I wasn't going to succumb to my family's machinations. There was no romantic future for us, and I just wanted to be left in peace to take on the job I was doing here." Even thinking back now, I was proud of my direct, straightforward delivery.

"And it worked?" She cracked the eggs into the bowl and gave them a stir into the mixture.

"It worked," I said. "He seemed to respect me for my up-front honesty. And then we had sex."

"I'm so glad—" Katie's expression fell. "Wait. *What?*"

"It was nothing—you know, not romantic in any way, just chemistry."

Her complexion flushed a little. "You had *sex* with *Joe?*"

"Yes."

"While explaining to him there was no chance of a romance between you two?"

I could see how she might misunderstand. "You kinda had to be there to—"

"Adeline."

"He dared me to kiss him." I realized how that sounded. "The point being it would prove we weren't attracted to each other."

She stared at me in condemning silence.

I explained some more. "It was a chemical thing. No hearts, no flowers, no romantic, candlelit lead-up or anything." I cast my memory back. "Well, there were candles on the table at dinner, but not like that."

"Why would you *do* that?"

"We got a little carried away." I supposed you could call it a lot carried away.

"No kidding."

"These are all mashed."

She hit the trigger on the mixer and finished blending in the eggs. Then she set the mixer aside and held out her hand for the bananas. "And what did he say?"

I moved to hand them over. "About what?"

"About the Dodgers. About *the sex*." She emptied the mashed bananas into the bowl.

"Oh, he understood." We'd been surprisingly in sync afterward.

"Are you sure? Bring over the flour."

I went for the big white bowl where we'd mixed flour, salt and baking powder. "I'm positive."

"You have to blend the wet with the dry quickly. Don't overmix," she said, demonstrating. "Grab the pans and give them a spray."

I doused the pans with nonstick spray and set them next to the mixing bowl.

"Now, what *exactly* did he say?" she asked.

"I don't remember exactly. He said it was great sex."

Katie's expression broke out in a grin. "Was it?"

"Yes." I searched my memory a bit more. "He also said it was nothing but pent-up sexual energy and he'd still support our financial ask for the project."

"Well, then." She looked amused as she spooned the batter into the pans.

"What's so funny?"

"In a million years, I never would have thought to use great sex to chase a man away. Open the oven."

I crossed the kitchen and opened the big-windowed door. "Neither would I."

Katie set the pans side by side on the top rack.

"But sometimes things just work out." I closed the door while she set the timer. "Wine while we wait?" I asked.

"You bet." She rinsed out the dishcloth and wiped the counters while I opened a bottle of merlot and poured.

We settled at the tiny kitchen table in an alcove overlooking the compact backyard.

She lifted her glass. "To great sex and men who support your financial asks."

I chuckled and clinked glasses. But when I brought the wine to my lips, a sour aroma suddenly invaded my nostrils. "Hold it. I think this has turned." I took an experimental sniff.

Katie took a sip. "Tastes fine to me."

I wrinkled my nose. "Are you sure? This is off."

She drank again. Then she reached out. "Maybe it's your glass. Hand it over."

I did.

She took a sniff. "I don't know what you're talking about." She sipped. "This is perfectly fine wine."

I wondered if my palate had been permanently ruined by the bottle Joe and I had shared at the Forberg Club. That would be tragic. I didn't want to have to buy expensive wine for the rest of my life.

Katie was giving me an odd look.

"What?" I asked.

"When exactly did you and Joe have sex?"

"After the meeting. We came back here."

"What day?"

"I don't know, beginning of last week."

"Ten days? Twelve?"

I suddenly got where she was going, and my stomach lurched in horror.

"Adeline, are you pregnant?"

"No." I did some frantic math. "It's not—" I scrambled

for my phone and brought up a calendar, running my fingertip along the weeks. "There. See. I'm—" I looked back up at Katie. "Five days late."

She groaned and did a forehead plant into her palm.

Three hours and one pregnancy test later, Katie and I were in the living room staring at each other in silence for long stretches. She'd finished both our glasses of wine while I'd gone with a cup of lemon tea. It tasted better anyway.

"I shouldn't have been ovulating," I said. "Like...no way."

"Sometimes it happens," she said.

I closed my eyes, trying to calm myself down.

After a minute, Katie spoke into the silence. "You okay?"

My mind was spinning. But reality was reality. I managed a small smile. "Maybe it will help if I say it out loud?"

"Say it out loud."

"I am having a baby."

Katie gave an understanding nod. "Okay. Right. We should ice the cake. It'll be cool by now."

"You've had two big glasses of wine," I pointed out.

"It's not illegal to ice a cake when you're over the limit."

I managed a wider smile.

"That a girl." She rose to her feet. "Keep your sense of humor."

I followed suit. "I can't exactly sit around and fret for the next nine months."

"I hope the cake at least tastes good to you," Katie said as we returned to the kitchen.

"I've finished my education." I was talking more to myself than her, telling myself to look on the bright side. "I can do a lot of my work from home. Daycares exist. Nannies exist." Being a single mother hadn't been part of my life plan yesterday, but it looked like it was now.

She poked experimentally at the butter and cream cheese that were softening in the mixing bowl. "I could stay in Alaska, help out."

"You have a good teaching job that you've spent eight years working for."

"I know. But I can't leave you here all alone."

"I won't be alone in about eight months." I was frankly surprised at my ability to make a baby joke this soon. I felt a little bit proud of that.

Katie returned my smile. "It's softened. And it's dairy—good for you."

"Probably the bananas are, too."

"Potassium." She opened a bag of confectioners' sugar. "What are you going to tell Joe?"

"Just the facts." I tried to imagine Joe's reaction, but I had no frame of reference for him receiving unexpected news. I realized I'd only ever seen him in social situations. What if he had an unexpectedly bad temper?

"You going to call him in DC?"

"Maybe I'll just send a text."

"You *can't*." She looked at my expression and saw I was joking.

My phone rang just then, vibrating against the table where I'd left it earlier. For a split second, I was afraid it might be Joe. But it was my cousin.

"It's Sophie," I said to Katie, picking up and putting cheerful into my voice. "Hi, you."

"You're in Alaska?" Sophie sounded excited.

"You heard." I pretended it was no big deal, even as my heart sank. If Sophie knew, then the whole family knew.

"Yes! Joe told Mason he talked to you in Windward,

that you've got some big-deal construction project going on over there."

"That's where I am," I said, silently cursing Joe. So much for him keeping my secret. I didn't know why I'd thought I could trust him.

"So, when are you coming here? Want me to send Stone to pick you up?"

Nathaniel Stone was Sophie's new husband, a vice president at Kodiak Communications. Like my brothers, he had a pilot's license and used corporate planes to fly all over Alaska.

"Not yet," I said, planning to stall for as much time as possible. "My stuff was only just delivered today. The project is going full speed, and I've got all this unpacking."

"I understand," she said. "But I can't *wait* to see you."

"Me, too." Sophie was the person I'd most look forward to seeing in Anchorage.

Katie had paused on the other side of the kitchen and was pointing to the mixer.

I nodded and ducked around a corner in the hallway so she could make noise. "How's everyone there?" I asked Sophie.

"Braxton's behaving himself," she said on a laugh.

"What does that mean?"

"He's not bugging me for grandchildren this week."

My hand went subconsciously to my stomach, thinking that against all odds, I was going to be the first one to have a baby. It was no secret that both my father and his brother, Braxton, hoped for numerous grandchildren to perpetuate the family dynasty.

Braxton had lost hope of ever having any grandchildren until Sophie showed up last year, believing she had a long-lost cousin in Anchorage. No one was more stunned than her to discover she was Braxton's biological daughter. Now he could hardly wait for grandchildren, and Braxton wasn't one to be patient.

"Glad to hear it," I answered her.

"How'd it go with Joe?" she asked, trying hard to sound casual.

She knew about the family's matchmaking aspirations. Out of everyone, Sophie had the most sympathy for me. On the other hand, she really liked Joe and had suggested on more than one occasion that I give him a fair shot. Still, she was great, and I was lucky to have her as a cousin.

I wanted to tell her the truth. But I couldn't ask her to keep anything from Stone, so there was no way I was sharing. "He told me he'll help us get federal money. For the construction project, I mean. There's a program, but we need his support."

"Any catch?"

"No catch." Except for the fact that he'd outed me to my family. That was a catch I hadn't seen coming.

"Nothing?" She sounded skeptical about that.

"We did have dinner."

"And…?"

"It wasn't as bad as I expected." I was being honest, even if I was leaving some gaping holes in the information. Dinner had gone better than I'd expected. "He didn't propose marriage or anything."

He'd specifically not proposed marriage, for which I was grateful.

"You're paranoid, Adeline. He just wants to get to know you."

"Is that what Stone told you?"

"That's what Joe told me."

"Wait, you've been talking to Joe about me?"

Her tone turned airy. "People come to me for advice, Adeline. I can't help it if they trust me."

I was worried now that they'd co-opted Sophie to the cause. "What did you tell him?"

"To give you space."

I blew out a sigh of relief. "Thanks."

"Don't thank me. It's my true opinion. I honestly think that gives him the best shot with you."

I thought back to how Joe had behaved at dinner, very low-key and unassuming. It hadn't worked—at least, not completely. But I had let my guard down toward the end of the evening.

I could see now he'd been following Sophie's advice. Which could mean he hadn't given up yet—only given me the distance I craved as part of a strategy. Now, *that* was an unsettling thought.

"When do you think you'll have time to visit?" she asked.

"I'll have to play it by ear for a bit."

"Okay. I won't say I'm not disappointed. Make it soon, okay?"

"Soon as I can," I promised. "Say hi to everyone."

"Will do. Glad you're back."

I wasn't exactly glad, and I wasn't exactly back. "I'm excited about the project."

"Good. Talk later." Sophie signed off.

When I returned to the kitchen, Katie was smearing fluffy cream cheese icing on top of the two-layer cake. It looked delicious, and I couldn't wait to dig into a big slice.

"She knows you're here?" Katie asked, briefly glancing up.

"Joe told Mason, and Mason told Stone, and I'm sure the two of them will have told everybody. It's exciting news, me being back in the zone."

"I supposed it was inevitable." She finished with a flourish. "Cake?"

"Absolutely. But he said he wouldn't tell them." I was still grappling with my disappointment over Joe's betrayal.

"Did he mention the sex?"

I shook my head. If Sophie had heard I'd slept with Joe, it would have been the first thing out of her mouth. At least that part was still a secret.

Katie set the bowl and utensils in the sink.

I took two plates from the cupboard while she located a long, sharp knife.

"When are you going to tell him?" she asked as she cut generous slabs and set them on the plates.

I got us a couple of forks. "Seems like something I should do in person."

My number-one priority was to convey the information, but it was probably a good idea to see his expression when he reacted. I realized I had absolutely no earthly idea what to expect.

We carried our cake to the kitchen table.

"Is he coming back soon?" Katie asked.

"That seems unlikely." I took a bite of the cake. The moist sweetness exploded deliciously in my mouth. "Wow. That's fantastic. Where'd you learn how to cook like this?"

"My nana. She has a hundred recipes stored up inside her head. One day soon I'm going to write them all down."

"I want this one." As I said that, I realized how very unlikely it was that I'd have time to bake, especially now, especially with my life about to turn itself upside down. "A baby," I said, then I took another bite.

"It's hard to wrap your head around it."

"Impossible." I couldn't even picture my belly swelling up. I knew it would be weeks before that happened. But I also knew time had a way of slipping by.

It seemed like only yesterday that we'd graduated. And now we both had jobs. Katie had gone to California. Now she was back. We'd finished moving, and Joe had been here—twice.

"I have to go there to tell him." That much was certain. She nodded. "I agree."

I made a concrete decision. "Next weekend, quick turn-around to DC. I'll charter a jet."

Katie stared at me in silence for a beat. "I forget, you know."

"Forget what?"

"You act really normal all the time, and I forget you're so rich."

The money rarely mattered to me. "I don't often pull out the trust fund platinum card. But I think I will this time."

"Do you literally have a trust fund?"

"It's just shares of the company from my grandfather. But they pay dividends, and those tend to add up."

Katie coughed out a laugh. "*Tend to add up.* I know you're talking about significant money if you're flying private at the drop of a hat."

I shrugged. "The money just sits there."

"Until you need a jet."

"You want to come along?" I knew I would appreciate the company.

"Are we talking those huge white leather lounge seats and flutes of champagne?"

"I don't know if the seats will be white. But I'm looking for speed so, yes, that'll come with luxury."

"I'm in." She immediately sobered. "Sorry. I shouldn't be talking like this will be fun."

I didn't blame her. It might not be fun, but it was absolutely surreal. "At this point, it is what it is."

My hand went to my stomach again. I didn't know whether to laugh or cry or wail in frustration. I did know none of those things would change reality.

Four

I expected Joe to meet me in the reception area of his congressional office, since security had called up for permission to let me in the building.

But he wasn't there. The compact space was impressively opulent, with a small walnut desk, two tufted pale green guest chairs and a low table all arranged beneath tasteful oil paintings of Alaskan wilderness scenes. The receptionist sat against the wall with a closed door beside her.

"You must be Dr. Cambridge," the thirtysomething woman said as I paused inside the doorway. She wore a burgundy wraparound coatdress with a slim skirt, a wide fabric belt and oversize buttons decorating the collared vee neckline.

Along with being nervous, I now felt underdressed in my cropped black pants and fall leaf–patterned blouse. Since it was a half mile walk from the hotel, I'd stuck with low-heeled sandals with gray leather cross-ties. I'd thought the look was neutral, but now it struck me as halfway between smart casual and pool deck.

I hadn't calmed down any on the walk over, so half of me was dying to turn and run. "Adeline," I said. "Please call me Adeline."

"The congressman is finishing up a meeting."

"I don't mind waiting." It felt like a reprieve. Maybe I'd be able to get myself together before his meeting ended.

The door beside her suddenly opened, and Joe appeared. "Adeline." He sounded half surprised and half worried.

"I'm sorry to bother you," I said.

"No. Not at all." He looked to the receptionist. "Bree, can you cancel my ten thirty?" Then he gestured me inside. "Come on in."

"I can be quick," I said as I started his way.

"Did you come all this way to lobby for the project?"

"Not exactly."

"Do you need something? Can I help?"

"I have some news," I said but then decided that didn't sound right. "I have an update."

"Great." He sounded happy now, even eager.

I was sure about to change all that. I walked through the door to his inner sanctum.

His desk was gleaming cherrywood with two matching guest chairs covered in padded dark green leather. His art echoed the paintings in the reception area, while a small meeting table took up one corner. It was surrounded by four wooden chairs. The only other furniture were two compact armchairs sitting together under the window. Joe went there and gestured for me to sit down.

As I sat, my stomach did rapid flip-flops. I wished I'd had a few more minutes out in the reception area to compose my speech. Everything I'd thought of last night sounded terrible inside my head right now.

"What's up?" he asked, leaning forward.

I resisted an urge to draw back like a coward. Instead, I squared my shoulders. Then I swallowed.

He cocked his head. "Has something gone wrong?"

I managed a tight little nod, ordering myself to say something—anything.

His brow furrowed. "Adeline?"

"I'm pregnant," I blurted out. Then I clamped my jaw, not quite believing I'd said it so bluntly.

Joe didn't react, and I wondered if the shout had been inside my head.

Then his brow lifted, and his eyes got round.

"I didn't mean for it to come out like that," I said.

It took him another second to speak. "I'm not sure leading up slowly would have helped."

"I wanted to tell you in person."

He opened his mouth again but then closed it without speaking.

I knew I had to be patient. I'd had a week to get used to this, where he'd had a full thirty seconds.

"I can leave you alone," I offered, half rising.

His hand shot out to stop me, touching my thigh. "No. Don't leave. Don't—"

I sat back down.

We both sat in silence for a few minutes.

"I just wanted to let you know," I said.

"You came all this way?"

"Nothing needs to change. Definitely not right away. We can carry on as normal." I had months left before the pregnancy would even be obvious.

"Normal?"

"I get there'll be long-term decisions, but right now—"

"Who else knows?"

"Just my friend Katie."

"Is she trustworthy? Will she tell anyone?"

"She won't tell anyone." I wanted to make a snide remark about him not turning out to be so trustworthy, about him telling my family I was in Alaska after he'd promised he wouldn't.

"What about your family?"

"Why would she tell my family?" Katie hadn't ever met my family.

"We need to tell your family."

I stood then. "Oh, no, no, no. I already heard from Sophie."

He rose with me, looking baffled. "You just said they didn't know."

"About my being in Alaska," I clarified.

"What about it?"

"You told Mason."

"So?"

"I *asked* you not to." I didn't know why I was diverging from the main topic, but I was still annoyed that Joe had almost immediately betrayed my confidence.

His voice rose a little. "You meant about being in Alaska? I thought you meant about having sex."

"Both."

"Well, you didn't make that clear. You thought they wouldn't notice you were in Alaska?"

"They noticed really fast when you *ran to them* with the gossip."

"It wasn't gossip. It was a casual conversation, a topic of mutual interest. I really thought you meant the sex."

"Fine," I said, deciding to believe him on that point.

"We have to tell them about the baby."

I took a step backward, waggling my finger at him, coming up against the chair. "Oh, no, we don't. Not yet."

"As soon as possible."

"I've got plenty of time." I wanted a plan, an outline

for my life, for what it was going to look like as a single mother before I let my well-meaning but interfering father and the rest of them in on the discussion.

"I'm not keeping something like this from Xavier and Braxton."

"*You* wouldn't be keeping it from them."

But Joe was nodding. "That's my baby—" His gaze dropped to my stomach, and his entire demeanor changed. Reality seemed to have hit him in a wave. His voice dropped lower. "This is my responsibility."

I might have gown angry or laughed at the thoroughly dated concept, but it was easy to see he was wrapping his head around the magnitude of our situation.

"Don't panic," I said.

He met my gaze. "Panic? This isn't panic. This is recognition that my relationship with your family is very important to me."

That wasn't exactly news. "Don't worry. They'll still support you."

He flinched. "That's not what I—"

"I don't hold your priorities against you. Hey, I had dinner with you to finance a public project. That was hardly a noble move on my part."

He looked annoyed now. "I don't care about me. I care about them. I respect them both. I'm not going to lie about something this important, and I'm not willing to spring it on them at the last minute."

"They're going to be happy, Joe. No matter how it happened, this is a grandchild, the next generation. There will be champagne corks popping all over the Cambridge mansion when they get word of this."

"So, there's no downside," he said, a subtle but calculating expression on his face. "To telling them now?"

"Now? *Now?* What do you mean, now?"

"When are you going back to Alaska?"

I hadn't decided exactly. The private jet company only needed three hours' notice. "Soon."

"Good. I'm coming with you."

"There he is," Katie said while we waited on board the jet at ExBlue Executive Airport.

Joe's sleek black car had stopped outside on the tarmac. He rose from the back seat and retrieved his suitcase from the open trunk.

I watched his lithe movements as he closed it and headed for the plane.

"If your baby has to have a father…" Katie said, craning her neck in the rear-facing seat to see through the rounded window.

"You mean genetically speaking?" I wasn't about to argue against that.

"He's definitely got the looks and athleticism," Katie said.

"It's the arranged-marriage vibe that stops me cold."

Katie grinned and sat back in her seat, facing me. "I hear you. I can only imagine who my parents would pick for me—an accountant or maybe a dentist."

"You have something against accountants and dentists?"

"Too precise, too rules oriented, no imagination."

"You're a physicist."

"Astrophysicist. That means I can deal with unknowns, hypotheses and speculation."

I held up my palms in surrender. "Don't worry. I'm not trying to pick your husband."

She waved as Joe stepped onto the plane. He handed off his suitcase to the male attendant, then leaned into the cockpit.

Katie leaned toward me. "I want someone exciting."

"Maybe you shouldn't work at a university. Lots of tweed and uptight in the faculty there."

She seemed to consider that fact.

Joe turned my way then, a bright smile on his face. He'd obviously had a satisfying conversation with the pilots. Maybe they were based in Alaska. If so, they might be voters. He could have taken the opportunity to chat them up.

"Morning," he said, ducking slightly under the low ceiling as he walked, then swung into the seat across the aisle from me.

There was a seat facing Joe's, plus two more and a sofa behind us. Behind that was a restroom.

"Joe, you remember my friend Katie," I said.

Joe quickly offered his hand. "Nice to see you again, Katie."

"Likewise," she said as he sat back and settled in.

The attendant came down the aisle to stand between us. "Would anyone care for a drink after takeoff?" he asked.

Joe looked to me.

"Orange juice if you've got it," I said.

"Of course, ma'am." He looked to Katie next.

"Mimosa?"

"Certainly."

"Coffee for me, please," Joe said. "Black is fine."

"Coming up shortly," the man said. "We're about to begin our taxi. Can I ask you to please buckle up?"

We all reached for our seat belts while the jet engines' pitch went higher and louder outside our windows. The sound subsided a bit as we started forward, trundling toward the runway.

We lifted off and climbed fast. The jet had a lavish interior, but it was predominantly built for speed and would get us to Alaska in under five hours. As it leveled out, the attendant made his way back, a silver tray balanced on one hand.

"Mimosa," the man said to Katie, setting a crystal flute on a small napkin in front of her, making me just a little bit jealous.

"Orange juice," he said next.

The juice was in a tall, frosty glass with plenty of ice. It looked freshly squeezed and delicious. I felt a bit better about it.

"Coffee for you, sir." The man put a tall black mug on the table in front of Joe. "I'll be making French crepes for breakfast, if that's acceptable. Standard bacon, eggs and toast are also available. I'll give you a few minutes to decide."

We were headed for Anchorage, where we'd pick up a rental car and drive straight to the family's mansion. We didn't have any time to waste since I had to be at work Monday morning.

Overnight, I'd come around to Joe's way of thinking. The more time my family had to get used to the idea of a baby, the better it was for everyone. It would be selfish to keep it to myself just because I was nervous.

I wasn't that nervous. Single moms weren't a big thing anymore. Sure, some pregnancies were accidental, but many single women simply decided it was time to have a family. Who was to say I wasn't one of those?

Not that I'd tell my family this was planned. I'd be straight with them. No matter the circumstances, I was certain the baby would be treated as extremely happy news.

"You should take an extra day," Joe said, as if he'd guessed where my thoughts had gone.

I shook my head. "I'm not asking for a personal day this early in my tenure."

"Why not?"

"Because it would be unprofessional."

"Do you *want* to stay over in Anchorage?"

I thought about Sophie and how nice it would be to have a visit with her. "Sure. But I'm not going to ask."

"I could ask."

"Oh, no, you don't."

"Why not? It's a big deal."

"You can't pull rank on William."

"I won't lie," Joe said. "I'll just tell him we'll be meeting there."

It felt wrong, but I was tempted. I looked to Katie for a second opinion, and she shrugged.

"William?" I heard Joe ask.

I whirled my head his way and saw he was already on the phone. *"You're not,"* I hissed.

He gave me a wink. A *wink*, like we were conspiring together to ditch gym class or something. "Joe Breckenridge here. How are things with you?"

I looked back at Katie, who seemed amused by the turn of events.

"I'm very well, thank you," Joe said. "Listen, could you possibly spare Adeline on Monday? I'm going to be in Anchorage, and I was hoping to meet with her. She can visit her family while she's there."

I was more than nervous now and shook my head at Joe, making a slashing motion across my throat.

"I am," Joe said easily. "I will. Thanks, William, appreciate that." Joe ended the call.

"You—" I didn't even know what to say.

"William is thrilled. He sees it as another chance for you to co-opt me. Which it is."

"I don't have to co-opt you. You're already on board. And I already told him that."

"In politics, there's always room for more schmoozing.

Look at it this way, you might be in Anchorage, but you're still working for the good of the project."

My phone rang then. I checked the screen and saw it was William.

I put a finger to my lips for quiet and took the call. "Hello, William."

"Adeline," he opened heartily. "Good that I caught you."

"I know, I'm here with—"

"There's been a development." William sounded rushed. I hoped he wasn't annoyed. "Yes, the congressman—"

"The governor's flat-out defecting, and it looks like the senator's in play." William had seemed unflappable up to now. But he was clearly agitated. "Congressman Breckenridge's support is more vital than ever. If he wants you in Anchorage, then *I* want you in Anchorage."

"What changed?" I asked, earning me curious looks from both Joe and Katie.

"I'm trying to figure it all out. There's been a budget cut in the fund and Governor Harland pledged his support for the road extension. He's leaning heavily on the senator to support him. It seems like Nigel's in thick with the senator's staff, so you need to talk to the congressman. You know what to do?"

My gaze went to Joe, who was watching me with open curiosity. "I think so."

"Don't lose him, Adeline. He's our last hope."

"He's already—"

"We need *more* than just Breckenridge on our side. We need Breckenridge to keep Senator Scanlon on our side, or we can pack it all up and try again in two years."

It had been months since I'd been home.

My brother Mason was in the great room when we walked through the front door, and his smile beamed as soon as he saw me. A split second later, he frowned. "What did you do to your hair?" But he came straight over and pulled me into a warm hug, just like he always did. After a second, he pulled back, apparently to confirm it was really me under the short blond locks. "Did you lose a bet?"

"I'm fine. Don't you like it? I was in the neighborhood."

He grinned again and then glanced past me—doing a double take at Katie, I presumed, given the goofy expression that came over his face.

I turned to her. "This is my friend Katie Tambour from Sacramento—well, my housemate right now. Katie, this is my brother Mason."

Mason moved her way, offering his hand. "Welcome to Alaska, Katie."

The melodic tone of interest in his voice was embarrassing. But Katie was gorgeous, so I wasn't surprised.

"Nice to meet you, Mason," she said, and I could hear the note of humor. My brother wasn't the first guy to turn sappy on her.

"Joe?" Mason sounded surprised now. "What…? Where…?" He looked around the circle at the three of us. "Something up?"

"We landed at the same time," I said without elaborating.

"I'm enjoying Alaska very much so far," Katie said, pulling Mason's attention away from Joe.

I knew it was deliberate, and I silently thanked her for being my wingperson again.

"The air," she continued. "You should advertise the clean air in your tourism ads. You all must have the best lungs in the world."

Mason drew in a breath—seeming to test her hypothesis.

"Adeline?" It was my brother Kyle now, slightly younger but almost a copy of Mason. He also pulled me into a warm hug. "I like it," he said, ruffling my short hair. "Way to go bold."

After the hug I watched him take in Katie.

"Who's this?" But his attention quickly switched again. "Hey, Joe. I didn't know you were coming."

"Last-minute decision," Joe said, shaking Kyle's hand.

"Kyle, this is my friend Katie Tambour from California." I made the introduction a second time. "Katie, this is my other brother, Kyle."

"Hello, Katie from California." He glanced around at the small group. "Are we having a party or something?"

"Adeline!" It was Sophie calling out this time. "I *love* it!" She dashed in for a hug while Stone sauntered in behind her.

"Nice color," she said. "Nice cut." She bent sideways to look around me.

"What's all the commotion?" My uncle Braxton's voice shifted the atmosphere a little bit. "Adeline? Well, it's about time you dropped in. Does your dad know you're here?" He didn't say a word about my hair.

"We just got here," I said. I went to Braxton and gave him a more perfunctory hug.

"You brought Joe?" There was curiosity in his tone.

"Joe brought himself," I said.

Joe strode over. "Nice to see you again, Braxton. I'm on the periphery of Adeline's project down in Windward."

"That arts thing?" Braxton asked. His gaze switched back and forth between the two of us. It was quite annoying the way he tried to read minds—even more annoying that he was so good at it.

"It'll be a big complex—national money, significant impact on the economy of the region," Joe said.

Braxton looked satisfied by that answer, and I silently thanked Joe for distracting my uncle.

"I brought a friend along," I said to Braxton.

Braxton gave Katie a polite nod. "Kyle, let Sebastian and Marie know we have guests."

"Happy to," Kyle said and headed for the kitchen.

"How long will you be staying?" Braxton asked me.

"Just a couple—"

"Adeline?" It was my father, Xavier.

I turned to face him. "Hi, Dad."

He was frowning instead of smiling, and I wondered if he was about to question my new haircut. "What's wrong?"

I touched the back of my hair. "Nothing."

"You sure?" He took in Joe and Katie.

"I convinced her it was time to visit," Joe said.

"Joe's funding Adeline's little project in Windward," Braxton said.

"It's more than a *little* project," I said, annoyed at the characterization even though I was glad to switch topics. I also wasn't thrilled by their presumption of Joe's benevolence.

My dad's hug was slightly warmer than Uncle Braxton's, but still more reserved than most.

"We always appreciated the congressman's help," my dad said, the hug over quickly. "Nice to see you again, Joe."

"Happy to be here," Joe said.

"Let's get Katie settled," Sophie put in, for which I was grateful.

"Good idea," I quickly agreed, moving with Sophie toward the grand staircase and motioning for Katie to come along.

She sidled up to me and whispered in my ear. "You actually *live* here?"

I saw Sophie smile.

"I used to," I said as we walked.

Katie took in the high ceilings, the multiple cream-colored leather furniture groupings in the great room, the stone fireplace and the wall of glass that showed off the backyard.

"It's like a hotel," she said in awe.

"I felt the same way the first time I saw it," Sophie said, mounting the wide staircase. "You'll love the guest room."

"So, you didn't grow up here?" Katie asked Sophie.

"Not even close. An apartment in Seattle."

"But she got rich all on her own," I put in.

"Not this kind of rich," Sophie said with a laugh.

"No wonder you're chartering jets," Katie said.

Sophie gave me a look. "Jets?"

Katie flashed me a silent apology.

"We were in a hurry. Turns out the governor's supporting a competing project." I rattled on with unnecessary information, hoping to distract Sophie. "And the governor's trying to co-opt the senator, and my boss wants me to get Joe to hit up the senator to support us instead."

We came to the top of the stairs.

"Well, you can get Joe to do anything you want," Sophie said. "We can all see how he feels about you."

This time Katie shot me an amused grin.

"Here's the guest room," I said to her, opening the door with a flourish.

Katie took two steps inside and stopped.

I tried to see it through her eyes—the high ceilings and exposed beams, the banks of windows along two walls. The floor was natural wood, highlighted by a plush, forest green area rug. It wasn't all that much different than my room, since the same decorator had designed them both.

Out of practicality, the room had a king-size four-poster bed. The windowed corner held a conversation area with a sofa, two plush, overstuffed armchairs and a couple of glass-topped tables, while a marble-framed gas fireplace took up most of one wall and a dressing and closet area led into a bathroom with a soaker tub, a separate shower and dual sinks.

Sophie slipped past Katie to watch her expression.

"Been there," Sophie said with a laugh.

Katie moved forward and spun around. "This is…mind-blowing."

"Pro tip," Sophie said. "When Marie insists on doing your laundry, just say yes. Life is simpler that way."

"We won't be here that long," Katie said.

Sophie looked at me, her brow arched in a question.

"I have to be at work on Tuesday," I said. "In fact, this is work. My big objective for tomorrow is to secure Joe's support on the senatorial front."

Sophie looked confused. "You're joking, right? How long does it take to crook your little finger?"

Katie stifled a laugh.

"Things have gotten weird," I said. I didn't want to tell Sophie the pregnancy news before anyone else, but I didn't want to stand here and pretend everything was status quo, either.

"Weirder than usual?" she asked. "I mean, you're here, Joe's here, your dad and Braxton are here. The three of them together always make you jumpy."

"True," I agreed. "I've seen more than I expected of Joe over the past few weeks."

Sophie looked happy to hear it. "Are you warming up to him?"

I hesitated, trying to frame up something that was true but not too revealing.

"I told her to be straight with him," Katie put in. "All this tippy-toeing around wasn't doing anyone any good."

"What did you say?" Sophie asked, looking disappointed.

"It's obvious he's co-opted you now," I said back.

"I like him, too," Katie said.

I gave her a look that said she was a traitor.

She gave me her favorite shrug. "You said it yourself—everyone likes him."

"Because he's a good guy," Sophie said. "You have reverse Romeo and Juliet syndrome."

I tried to glean her meaning. "Reverse—"

Katie jumped in. "Your parents push you together, and you throw yourselves apart."

"I don't think that's a thing," I said.

"It sounds plausible to me," Katie said.

"Whose side are you on?"

"Yours." She moved to rub my shoulder. "Completely yours."

Our gazes met, and I knew we needed to get the big reveal over with.

"We should go downstairs," I said.

"Okay, but we're having girl talk after dinner," Sophie said emphatically.

"Guaranteed," I said, knowing that much was true.

I hadn't purposely waited until dinner, but there were a lot of different conversations going on around the house, and I couldn't seem to corral everyone together until then.

I let Sebastian pour me a glass of red wine, intercepting a shocked look from Joe. I gave an imperceptible shake of my head to tell him I wasn't planning to drink it. But if I'd said no to wine, I would have drawn attention to myself. I didn't want that just yet.

Then Sophie turned down wine in favor of ice water, and I realized I could have gotten away with it.

"A toast," Braxton said from one end of the table. "Welcome home, Adeline. Nice to meet you, Katie. And welcome back, Joe."

We all raised our glasses, and I pretended to drink.

"I need to tell you something," I said before the separate conversations could start up again.

Joe was seated across the table, and I suddenly wished he was beside me for moral support. I knew it was silly. Having him closer wasn't going to change a thing.

"Yes?" my dad prompted. He was at the opposite end of the table from Braxton, cornerwise to me.

"I'm…" I looked at Joe.

He seemed calm.

I took a breath. "Pregnant."

There was a moment of surprised silence. I'd expected that.

"No way," Sophie called out, sounding totally delighted. She hopped up from her chair between Stone and Joe and rushed around the table to give me a rocking hug.

"A grandchild?" my dad said, sounding proud.

"Wait," Mason said. "Didn't we miss a few steps here?"

I knew it was a natural question, and I knew I had to answer, but I wanted to bask in Sophie's unbridled joy for a moment or two longer.

"The baby is mine," Joe said.

Most froze in surprise.

Braxton beamed. "Congratulations, son!"

My father reached for my hand and gave it a squeeze. "This is *wonderful* news."

"Why didn't you spill earlier?" Sophie demanded on a laugh, still hugging me.

I met Joe's gaze as we both realized our mistake.

Sebastian had apparently overheard the excitement, because he walked into the dining room carrying two bottles of champagne on a silver tray. His efficiency was unsettling.

"Dad, no," I quickly said in a firm voice. "It's not what

you think. We're not—" I waggled my finger back and forth between me and Joe. "We're *just* having a baby together. *That's all.*"

Everyone stopped talking and stared at me, clearly looking for an explanation.

My dad's eyes narrowed as he turned his head to Joe. "What does she mean, just a baby?"

Joe stepped up. "Adeline and I had a date, one date."

"You're not getting married?" Kyle asked.

"You're not engaged?" Mason looked at my hand.

"What do you mean, you're not getting married?" Braxton demanded thunderously.

Sebastian stepped lithely back out of the room.

Sophie's arm loosened a little around my shoulder.

"You'd better be diamond ring shopping," my dad said to Joe on a growl.

"It's not Joe's fault." I didn't want them turning on him. I could feel Katie's astonished stare at my left side. I was thinking twice about making her sit through this.

"You're having his baby," my dad said.

"We didn't want to spring it on you—"

"This feels pretty springy," Mason said.

"—at the last minute," I finished. "We just found out. We don't know what it means for the future."

"Well, *I* know what it had better mean for the future," Braxton said.

"Braxton," Joe said. Then he looked at my dad. "Xavier. I will do whatever Adeline wants, up to and including marrying her."

I glared at him, angered by his bait and switch. He was saving himself and throwing me to the wolves.

"But for now," he told them firmly, "*back off.* This is Adeline's decision, and hers alone. You are *not* going to push her into something she doesn't want to do." His hard gaze included Mason and Kyle. "Hear me? All of you?"

There was muttering and nodding among the group.

"I'm still thrilled," Sophie whispered in my ear.

I gave her arm a squeeze. Now that it was out in the open, I felt a bit of a thrill myself. It felt more real, like there really was a baby in my future—a *baby*.

Katie reached out to me then, touching my shoulder.

My gaze met Joe's, and I gave him a tentative smile. He'd had my back against my family. I didn't remember anyone ever doing that before.

"Hey," Sophie whispered even more softly in my ear. "Nobody knows, but I'm pregnant, too."

I turned to stare at her in open astonishment.

A glint in her eyes, she backed away a couple of steps and returned to her seat beside Stone, who squeezed her hand and gave her a kiss on the hairline. Love shone from his eyes.

The cooking staff began quietly and unobtrusively serving a summer greens salad.

I caught Sophie's gaze again and gave her a little nod. I wanted her to share her good news. She cocked her head in a question to confirm what I was saying, and I nodded again.

She leaned over and whispered to Stone, who looked at me as well.

I smiled at him with pure happiness.

Holding Sophie's hand, he spoke up. "Not to be outdone, but Sophie and I have news, too."

Everyone's attention went to him, and the servers discreetly pulled back.

"We are also expecting a baby." He raised Sophie's hand to his lips and gave her a kiss.

Braxton jumped to his feet and went to Sophie as congratulations erupted all over again. This time there was no bad news trailing it to cause a scene.

Braxton hugged his daughter, and I thought I saw a glimmer of tears in his eyes. I was reminded that only a year ago he'd believed he'd never have grandchildren. My heart squeezed with joy.

Sebastian reappeared with the champagne while another cook set flutes of ginger ale in front of Sophie and me.

Katie leaned over to whisper to me. "You okay?"

"I'm good. Sophie gave me a heads-up. This'll distract everyone."

"I hope so," Katie said, accepting a glass of the champagne. "They seem as single-minded as you told me."

"I know. But Joe helped." I looked his way again and found his gaze on me.

He sent me a *you okay?* chin dip, raising his brow.

I nodded. Sophie and Stone's happiness wasn't a negative for me, not in any way.

Braxton rose, lifting his flute of champagne. "To our expanding family."

People roundly echoed his words with cheers.

Five

"Girl talk is much more fun with wine," Sophie complained, staring at her glass of ginger ale.

"Sorry," Katie said, sounding guilty.

The three of us had settled on padded Adirondack chairs on the shared balcony between my bedroom and Sophie's old room overlooking the backyard and the horse paddock. Katie was the only one with a glass of wine.

"So, what is your plan?" Sophie asked me. "Short term, I mean. Next few months."

"Get the community on board with the preliminary plans, push for federal funding, figure out how to neutralize Nigel Long. He's in tight with the senator's staff."

"So, your instincts were right," Katie said.

"Who's Nigel Long?" Sophie asked.

"He works for the governor. He pretended they were in favor of the arts and culture center, but they double-crossed us when the funding ran short."

"What are you going to do about it?"

"We've scheduled sector meetings and public meetings. The arts pitch is an easy one—who doesn't want more artistic undertakings in their community? But now we have to fight on the economic front. We'll have to frame up the tourism opportunities, artisan exports, improved quality of life in Windward that would attract entrepreneurs, tech and otherwise."

"So, nothing babyish, then?" Sophie said.

My hand went to my stomach as I once again thought of the life growing there. "I don't expect there will be much to do for a while."

"I've already been shopping for maternity clothes," Sophie said.

"How many weeks are you?" Katie asked.

"Nine."

"You're ahead of me. I think I'm five, based on how the charts say to count it, anyway. I have an appointment with my doctor next week."

"That is early." Sophie looked concerned. "You told us really early."

"Joe was worried. He didn't want to keep it from Braxton and Xavier."

Sophie looked thoughtful. "They're not going to give up now, you know, wanting you two to be together."

I gave a dry chuckle at the understatement. "I've known those two men my entire life. They're regrouping."

"Joe was good at dinner, though," Sophie said.

I agreed with a nod.

"Do you think it was a ruse?" she asked.

"I don't think so," Katie put in. "I mean, I've only just met Joe, but he doesn't strike me as underhanded."

Neither Sophie nor I responded to the statement.

"You think he *is*?" Katie asked in obvious astonishment.

"There's a lot at stake," I said. "For Kodiak Communications and for Joe."

"It's a mutually beneficial arrangement," Sophie said.

"For Adeline to *marry* Joe?" Katie frowned.

"For Braxton and Xavier to be in tight with the congressman."

"And for him to be in tight with them," I said.

"You've made yourself perfectly clear," Katie said. "You'll do what you want to do, regardless of what they'd like."

"I know. They know that, too."

"But they will try to push you two together," Sophie said.

I wished I could keep a step or two ahead of them. But I'd never been able to do that.

The door to Sophie's old room opened and closed, and I leaned back to see who it was.

Kyle sauntered out onto the balcony.

"You do know this is girl talk," I said to my brother.

"I'd rather visit with this generation than the old, stodgy one," Kyle said, sitting down in an empty chair.

"We're talking about babies," Sophie warned.

"I like babies," Kyle said. He had a glass of wine in his hand, and he took a drink. "I can't wait to be an uncle."

I suspected he wanted to chat Katie up.

The door opened again, bringing Mason inside.

"I knew the party would be up here," he said, sitting himself down on the last empty chair. "What are we talking about?"

"Babies," Sophie said. "You two sure you want in on this? It might get icky."

"You think I wouldn't change a diaper?" Kyle asked.

"He wouldn't change a diaper," Mason said.

"Sure would."

"The topic was cute maternity tops," Sophie said in a singsong voice. "With polka dots and flowers—"

"And kittens," Katie added in a lilting tone. "Don't forget the kittens."

"Kittens," Sophie affirmed.

I couldn't help but smile as the wind came out of my brothers' sails.

Mason rallied first. "So, you're not pregnant, Katie?"

"I am not," she said and took a pointed sip of her wine.

"What is it you do down in California?"

"Teach," she said, "Soon, anyway. At Cal State."

"See, this is interesting," Mason said to Sophie. "And what is it you're going to teach at Cal State?"

"Astronomy." I raised my glass in a toast to her.

Mason looked surprised. "You can take that at Cal State?"

"Indeed."

"Isn't it a tier-one school?"

"So?"

He shrugged. "Okay." He paused for a second. "Well, I'm a Taurus."

Katie didn't miss a beat. "So, bullheaded."

He smiled. "That's cute. What else can you tell me?"

"You mean, like your future?"

I knew this wasn't the first time someone had gone off on an astrology tangent with Katie. Clearly, she was going to roll with it.

She set down her wineglass. "I'll have to see your palm." She motioned him over.

"Really?"

"Yes."

"Never heard of that before." But Mason rose and held his right hand out to her.

"Hmm," she said, running her finger along the creases

of his hand. "Oh, my." She looked up at him. "Have you ever had this done before?"

"No."

"Did you read your horoscope this morning?"

"No."

I looked at Sophie and saw her pinch her lips tight together. She was obviously fighting off laughter.

Kyle didn't look amused. If anything, he looked a little jealous.

"Anything go wrong today?" Katie asked Mason, a faux-concerned expression on her face.

He shifted, perching himself on the wide armrest of the chair. "No, why?"

"Oh, well." Katie looked at her watch. "I guess there's still time."

"*Here* you all are." Stone walked onto the balcony, bee-lining for Sophie.

He took her hand, helping her to her feet, then sat down and pulled her onto his lap.

Joe came in next and took the chair Mason had abandoned.

"Can we stave it off?" Mason asked Katie, staring at his hand, his expression worried. "Maybe sing a song or chant something?"

Joe looked to me and nodded their way. "What's she doing?"

"Telling his fortune, I think," I answered.

"She does that?" Joe looked lost.

"She's an astrologer," Mason said without turning.

"I'm an astronomer," Katie corrected.

"That's an astrophysicist," Stone told Mason.

"Well, that's a relief," Mason said. "I thought you were a legit fortune teller—that I was in real trouble."

I couldn't tell for sure if Mason had been genuinely confused or just playing along the whole time. Then his eyes lit up with amusement, and Katie tossed his hand back to him.

He turned to see he'd lost his seat to Joe.

"Mind if I share?" he asked Katie, squatting on the arm of her chair.

The look she gave him was incredulous. "I barely know you."

He held up his palm. "I already let you take a look at my secrets. I swear, I'm harmless."

Katie looked at me for confirmation.

"I'll vouch for my brother. I have indeed always thought of him as fairly harmless." I made a face at Mason, and he returned it.

Everyone laughed, and Katie settled back in her chair.

"How long are you staying?" Kyle asked me.

"It depends. Could be as long as two years."

"Here?" He pointed down at the deck, seeming surprised.

"In Alaska," I corrected. "If Joe works hard and we get all the funding we need."

"It's a huge project," Joe said. "Naturally, there are detractors."

"Can Kodiak Communications help?" Mason asked.

"Sponsorships," I immediately said. "There'll be some community fund-raising events in the fall. We'll have to get the bulk of the funding from Washington. And the state will kick in some. At least I hope they'll kick in some." Now that the governor had come out against us, that might be more of a challenge. "Raising community funds will demonstrate the level of public support."

"Congress doesn't mind investing public money," Joe added. He pulled a face then, making it obvious he was joking. "But we like to know it'll eventually translate into votes."

The group chuckled easily.

"So, we can expect to see more of you?" Mason asked me.

"Depends," I said.

"On Dad and Braxton?"

"On *all* of you."

"Feisty," Kyle said with a grin.

"Are you mocking me?" I asked him.

"Are you mocking her?" Joe asked from where he was seated next to Kyle.

"Wouldn't dream of it," Kyle said.

"Yes, I'll be home more often," I admitted. Now that they all knew I was here, and now that I'd made my position on Joe abundantly clear, it would be nice to visit more often.

"I have to go back for the fall," Katie said. "I'm a little bit sorry about that."

"Do you ski?" Mason asked her.

"I surf."

"Well, having good balance is half the battle. You can come back in the winter and try skiing."

"You say that like it's a hop, skip and a jump instead of cramming in a middle seat and transferring through LAX and SeaTac."

"There must be an easier way than that," Kyle said.

"Not if you want a discount fare."

"She lives in the real world," Sophie said. "I remember the real world."

"We're not going to let her fly coach," Mason said, sounding offended.

Katie turned to look at him, bracing her hand on the empty armrest. "*Let* me?"

"Allow me to rephrase," Mason said.

"Oh, do rephrase."

Joe looked amused, and I shared a smile with him.

Mason might not have been seriously flirting, but he was doing something.

"As our *guest*, we would expect to happily cover the cost of your transportation," Mason explained.

"You do that for all your guests?" Katie challenged.

"Hello?" Joe shook his head. "And here I've been buying my own tickets all these years?"

Mason shot him a narrow-eyed glare. "Not helping, Breckenridge."

"She'll come to visit me," I said, sounding purposely smug and self-satisfied.

"Her, I'll come to visit," Katie said, backing me up.

"But not me?" Mason asked, pretending to be offended.

"So far all you've done is steal the arm of my chair and mistake my profession."

"She's got you there," Stone said. "Anybody need another drink?" He took orders and left.

When he came back, he surprised Sophie and I with thick chocolate milkshakes.

"Oh, this is dangerous," I said, stirring the straw through a dollop of whipped cream. "I hope you thanked Sebastian for us."

"I did."

The conversation had broken into a few groups while Stone was gone. Katie and Mason had found something more agreeable to talk about, and she'd focused solely on him. Sophie had shared her plans with me for everything from prenatal vitamins to nursery decor. Joe and Kyle were talking about a new undersea backbone data cable that would connect Alaska overseas.

As I finished my milkshake, Joe moved my way. He crouched down beside my chair. "We should talk."

"We're heading in now," Stone announced, standing with Sophie.

Kyle came to his feet and stretched. "Me, too. Night, guys."

They all cut through Katie's guest room, and Joe pointed that we should go to mine.

"Got everything you need for tonight?" I asked Katie as I rose.

"I'm good." She started to move, but Mason's hand touched her hip, and she paused.

"See you in the morning," I said, leaving them to their conversation.

It was quiet in my bedroom. It felt intimate after the family dinner and the boisterous balcony conversation. My room was generously sized, with high ceilings, thick carpets, opaque blinds over the wide window, a gas fireplace and a bigger bed than I needed, plus a comfy sitting area.

"How are you doing?" Joe asked, his tone gentle as he moved in front of me.

I half expected him to take my hands in his, but he didn't.

"Fine," I answered. I was fine. I felt a little disoriented, but also like the worst was over.

"You know Braxton and Xavier won't stop pushing us together," he said.

"Did they say something?" I sure didn't want to have to fight the battle all over again tonight.

"Not to me."

"They need to accept reality. I was clear. *You* were clear. Thanks for that, by the way."

"You're welcome."

"I'm not used to someone standing up for me."

"That's because you've always been so independent."

"It's because the group of them, you included, have always wanted the same thing."

He seemed to contemplate my answer. "How old were you when your mom passed away?"

I was jolted by the sudden change in topic. "Twelve, why?"

"I was thinking you've been surviving in the world of men for a long time."

I didn't disagree with that. I remembered my sense of relief when Sophie showed up. I was so excited to have a female cousin, thrilled when she got together with Stone, because I knew that meant she was staying in our lives, my life, for the long term.

"Thank goodness for Sophie," I said.

"Thank goodness."

"Now that I've seen her, I wish I was staying a little longer."

"I can—"

"No, you can't." I put my hands on my hips and took a stance. "You can't use your power to corner my boss."

He looked amused. "I don't see why not."

"Because I'm an independent woman who can take care of herself, remember?"

"Okay."

"Don't you dare touch that phone."

"I won't."

"But speaking of my boss—"

"Hold that thought."

"You don't know what my thought is."

"I can guess. Before we go there…" He looked hesitant.

"What?"

"Can I—" He cast his gaze down to where the back of his hand hovered over my stomach. "Just for a second."

"Yes. Of course." I was touched that he wanted to.

He turned his hand, placing his palm against my abdomen. His palm was warm and tender, and we both stared silently.

"Nothing to feel yet," I finally said, my voice hushed.

"I know it's there. She's there? He's there?"

"We won't know that for quite a while." But the thought of a gender overwhelmed my emotions. I felt staggered and disoriented, and I reached for Joe's arm to steady myself.

"It's sinking in," he said, his hand still cradling my stomach.

"For me it's in waves. I'll get distracted and forget, and then I'll remember and panic." I gave a little laugh. "And then I'll feel happy, which will turn to scared, which will turn to excited. I'm all over the map."

He pulled me into a hug, and it felt wonderful. And then I felt flustered because it felt wonderful.

"You're not alone," he said.

I gently but firmly eased back from his embrace, worried I was letting my emotions cloud my judgment.

"This doesn't change anything," I cautioned him. I didn't want him to get the wrong idea. I didn't want him to think he could use this baby to pull me into a romantic relationship I was certain I didn't want.

"Adeline, it changes everything."

"I mean between you and me."

"So do I."

"Joe."

"Can I say something?"

"No." I could see in his expression and in his posture and hear it in his tone that he was going to take another run at a potential relationship between us.

"I'm going to say it anyway."

"Then why ask?"

"I don't know."

I braced myself. "Go ahead, but know up front that the answer is no."

"It could be temporary."

I shook my head.

"We could pretend, just for now, let the world know there's a you and me. That way, when the baby comes along, nobody is stunned, nobody is surprised, public opinion doesn't get rattled by something that seems like a secret or an accident or something unsavory."

My hackles rose, and my hand went protectively to my stomach. "This baby is *not* unsavory."

"I know that."

"Then why did you say it?"

"Have you *met* the general public? Because I've met them. They look for unsavory. They feast on unsavory. The more stability you give this baby, the more secure you make his or her future."

I could see what he was doing here. He was worried about his political career. And maybe he was right to be worried about his political career, since some people still judged men who didn't step up and marry the mother of their children. But I wasn't responsible for his political career, and our baby was not going to be some kind of good or bad publicity for his next election.

"We won't tell them," I said staunchly.

"Well, that'll make it worse. Because they will figure it out. They always figure it out eventually. And then you'll come under scrutiny along with me." He was a good orator, a great debater.

I knew I had to step back and regroup. "I'm not giving you a yes."

He smiled a little at that, and I could see the satisfaction in his eyes. "That's not a no."

"You feel like you won this round, don't you?"

He held his arms out as if surrendering. "There are no rounds, Adeline. There's just you and me, and we're both on the same side."

"Go," I said, because I could feel myself wavering.

Somewhere deep down inside I wanted to believe that, wanted to be on the same team as Joe. But I wasn't ready for that yet.

"Okay," he agreed with a nod, but instead of going straight for the door, he paused. "Sleep well." He touched my cheek, then he gently brushed his thumb across my lower lip, leaving a warm tingle in its wake.

And then, he was gone, the bedroom door closing behind him.

Breakfast was always a contrast in our house. My dad and Braxton were served formally in the windowed breakfast room off the back of the kitchen while the rest of us grabbed coffee and whatever yummy baked goods Sebastian and his team had on hand. We downed them in the kitchen—on our feet half the time—before rushing off to school or work. My brothers and I had started the habit as teenagers, and it carried forward to this day.

This morning there were cranberry scones and vanilla-glazed cinnamon buns in baskets on the counter. The scones were still warm, and I split mine open to spread it with butter.

"I'm not saying no to these," Katie said, setting a cinnamon bun on a little plate in front of her.

"Hop up," I told her, pointing to the six high swivel chairs around the central breakfast bar.

"Coffee?" Sophie asked us from where she stood in front of the built-in coffee maker. "Mocha, espresso, latte or, I suppose, coffee?"

"Mocha for me," Katie said.

"Latte," I answered, thinking it was never too early to move into better pregnancy eating habits. Between the dairy in my coffee and the vitamin C in the cranberries,

I hoped I was off to a decent start. I took the seat next to Katie.

Stone wandered in and helped himself to a scone.

"Coffee?" Sophie asked him.

"Go sit down," he said. "I've got it."

"Morning," Joe said from behind me.

I felt a warm shiver run up my spine. "Morning."

Sophie slid the mocha across the countertop to Katie.

"Anybody mind if I come and live here?" Katie asked as she popped a morsel of the cinnamon bun into her mouth.

"Plenty of room for everyone," Mason said as he walked in. "Where am I in the coffee lineup?"

"I'm making Adeline a latte," Stone said. "What'll you have?"

"Regular coffee." Mason slid on the seat on the other side of Katie. "I take it you liked the bed?"

"To die for," she said before popping another gooey bite in her mouth.

"Isn't it?" Sophie asked. "That was my room for a while. I don't know where they got that bed, but it's a dream."

"You want a new bed?" Stone asked Sophie.

"No."

"You like the guest bed better?"

"I like our bed just fine," Sophie said, rolling her eyes behind Stone's back.

"Because we can go shopping."

"Adeline?" My dad appeared in the entrance to the breakfast room. "Do you mind joining us for a minute?"

I could tell by the tone of his voice that they were about to pressure me again, and I reflexively looked to Joe. He might be more on their side than mine, but he was the closest thing I had to an ally.

"I'm coming, too," he said, steadying my elbow as I got down off the chair.

"Take this," Stone said, handing me my latte.

"You're a good man," I told him, joking in spite of the nervous flutter in my stomach.

As Katie had pointed out, I could always say no to whatever my dad and uncle asked. But they had a knack for making me feel guilty about it.

"Don't worry," Joe said in an undertone as we walked.

"I'm not worried," I lied. I'd known they wouldn't simply give up after last night, but this was pretty early in the morning for a second round of debate.

"Just give me a signal if you want me to pull you out." His tone made me smile.

"Like touch my nose and tuck my hair behind my ear?"

"That'll work." There was a thread of laughter in his voice, which I appreciated.

I sat down at the round breakfast table for eight with its white tablecloth, bone china and fresh flower arrangement. I took a spot partway around from my dad and Braxton. Then I took a sip of my latte.

"No pressure on her," Joe warned them as he sat down.

Braxton looked affronted. "This isn't about pressure."

"It's about logic and reason," my dad said.

"I have a job," I told them both, deciding to claim power by taking the lead. "It's a good job, and I'm excited about it. It's going to be my focus for the next couple of years."

My dad looked amused. "You don't think a baby's going to divert your focus?"

"I didn't mean that. I meant—" I canted my head toward Joe "—a relationship is not my priority right now."

"How do you know that?" Braxton asked reasonably. "A relationship can be a strength."

"Sure," I agreed. "When it's a real relationship."

My dad continued with the tag-team approach. "There are all kinds of relationships."

"Did you two rehearse this?" I asked.

"Don't deflect," my dad said.

"That's not an answer."

Braxton jumped back in. "We're only wondering if you've thought through the advantages, the numerous advantages of being with Joe."

"Stability," my dad said. "For you—"

"I'm already stable."

He gave me a warning with his narrowed eyes. "—for the baby, for the family."

There it was. "Please tell me you're not embarrassed about having a single mother in the family."

My dad looked genuinely affronted. "Of course not."

"Nobody cares about that," Braxton said.

"You seem to care."

They both shook their heads.

I was more convinced than ever that they'd rehearsed their arguments.

"You know why we've always supported a match between you and Joe," my dad said.

"Supported?" I raised my brows. "Is that what you call it? Don't you meant pushed? Planned? Orchestrated? Demanded?"

"Demanded?" Braxton asked and looked to Xavier. "That's a little strong, I think."

"You can't *will* me into Joe's arms." Everyone went quiet for a second, and I knew what they were all thinking—that I'd leaped eagerly into Joe's arms. "You know what I mean."

"We supported a match," Braxton said, "because of the strength it would bring both families."

My age-old resentment flared to life. "I'm not—"

"Let me finish, Adeline. For example, you said yesterday the senator isn't yet on board with your construction project. You said the governor had pulled his support. Unfortunately for you, the senator is going to support the governor. That's just how it has to work."

They were telling me my project was dead in the water. I hated to hear that, because they were likely right. They were always right about politics. They were crafty and smart, and they had their fingers on the pulse of the state. There was a reason Kodiak Communications had grown so big under their management.

"Adeline," my dad said. "If we were to announce your engagement to Joe—"

I started to object, but my dad kept talking.

"*If* we were to make that announcement and plan ourselves a big, splashy wedding, Senator Scanlon would step back and look at the chessboard."

I decided to bite. "What would the chessboard tell her?"

Joe sat forward. "That I was making a play to run for governor."

Both my dad and Braxton nodded.

"Are you in on this?" I demanded of Joe.

"No. I gave you my best reasons last night."

"She'd just *jump* to that conclusion, would she?" I asked all of them.

"Oh, she would," Braxton said. "We wouldn't have to say another word."

"And you do see her next logical move," my dad said.

Even I could see it. "Senator Scanlon rethinks her position on the arts and culture complex because Governor Harland has a real challenger in the next election."

"She's got it," Braxton said to my dad.

"That's—" I tried to think of the right word.

"Life in the major leagues," Braxton said.

"My reasons all still hold," Joe said to me.

"Marriage doesn't have to be forever," Braxton said.

"But it would sure smooth the way in the short term," my dad added.

"So, an actual wedding. As in, we'd really, truly get married." I couldn't believe I was considering it.

Losing the arts and cultural center would be a blow—both for me and for the citizens of Windward. It wasn't enough on its own to sway me. But Joe had made more sense than I'd been ready to admit last night. We needed to keep our baby, our child, out of the public fray.

"I live in DC most of the time," Joe said to me. "You'll be in Windward. We could easily stay out of each other's way."

I took in my father and uncle, barely accepting what my own sense of logic was telling me. "I can't believe this," I said out loud.

Confusion crossed both of their faces.

"You won," I told them in a quiet voice. "It all makes sense. I should marry Joe."

"Marry Joe?" Katie said with a frown.

"Marry *Joe*?" Sophie said with a wide grin.

"Marry Joe," I repeated, shaking my head.

We were at the horse paddock, and I leaned my elbows on the top rail. I'd needed some air and to get away from the house for a little while. Watching the horses had always been soothing.

"Okay, I *really* missed something," Katie said, the bright sun behind her, shadowing her expression.

"Joe's a great guy," Sophie told her, tucking her own golden-brown hair behind her ears in the light breeze. "I've seen quite a lot of him over the past year, and I really like him." She glanced at me. "Sorry."

"You don't have to take sides," I said. "I like him, too."

"Hello?" Katie glanced back and forth between us. "You cut your *hair* so he wouldn't find you."

Sophie was clearly baffled by the statement. "What does her hair have to do with Joe?"

"It's her disguise," Katie said, gesturing to me as if it was patently obvious.

I looped my fingers around a fence rail and leaned back. Since it hadn't worked, the disguise effort seemed amateurish now. "I was hoping to stay under the radar," I said. "You know, come back to Alaska without people noticing I was here. I figured new hair might help."

Sophie scoffed out a laugh. Then she sobered. "Wait, you're serious. Did it actually work on Joe?"

"Not for five seconds."

"Well, he's been thinking about you for most of the past decade. It'd take major cosmetic surgery or something to throw him off."

"I wore my glasses."

"I still like it, though," Sophie said, reaching out to brush my hair across my forehead. "I'm glad you did something dramatic."

"Back to the marriage?" Katie prompted as a pair of eagles soared past over the treetops. "Last I heard it was *a thousand times no.*"

A horse whinnied in the pasture, and the rest lifted their heads to look.

I tried to explain. "With the baby coming—"

"Have we time-warped here? You don't need to get married just because you're pregnant," Katie said.

"No, I see what she means," Sophie said. "Joe's in the public eye."

"What, deadbeat dad isn't a good look for the campaign?" Katie asked.

"It's not about Joe's political career," Sophie said with conviction. "Is it, Adeline?"

"More *because* of Joe's political career," I admitted.

"I'm not liking him so much anymore," Katie said with a frown.

"A baby's not noteworthy if the parents are together. If they're not, well, somebody's going to make it into a story."

"That is *not* a reason to get married."

"It doesn't have to be forever," I said, watching Splendor, a champagne horse and one of my favorites, walk toward us.

"Don't write Joe off like that," Sophie said.

"I'm going into this with my eyes wide-open," I said. Splendor shook her white mane. "And I get something out of it, too."

"Husbands aren't the prize they used to be," Katie said.

"My dad and Braxton said it'll make the senator think twice about pulling support for the arts and culture complex."

Sophie and Katie were both silent for a moment. A couple other horses followed Splendor.

"You've lost me," Katie said.

"Me, too," Sophie said to me. "Something we agree on here," she said to Katie.

Katie gave a smile.

"The two masters of machination think Senator Scanlon will read the engagement announcement, conclude Joe is going to make a run for governor and think about hedging her bets."

"You *believed* that?" Katie asked incredulously.

"No, it makes sense," Sophie said.

"It does." I was convinced they were right.

The horses grew closer. I wished I had some apples or carrots to share.

"Alaska's a lot like a small town," Sophie told Katie. "Everyone knows everyone. With the Cambridge brothers backing him, Joe would have a real shot at becoming governor."

"And *that's* what this has always been about," I said. "It's just never been in my interest to go along with it."

"So, you'd get the project funding," Katie said.

"If everything goes according to plan."

"Well, I guess I can buy into that as a reason."

"You're a mercenary," Sophie said to her.

"I'm pragmatic." Katie shrugged. "Same thing, I suppose."

Katie had her back to the fence, and I gently moved her forward before Splendor could nudge her shoulder and startle her.

"What?" Katie asked, and I pointed.

She turned and her eyes went round. "Where'd those come from?"

"Can I be a bridesmaid?" Sophie asked, petting Galahad's nose—a friendly chestnut gelding.

"Absolutely," I said. I scratched behind Splendor's ears.

Katie raised her hand and wiggled her fingers in the air. "Oh, me, too."

"Better do it soon." Sophie indicated her stomach. "If you want me to fit into the dress."

"Will the wedding be big and splashy?" Katie asked, looking like she was seriously warming up to the idea.

"I'd prefer the courthouse," I said honestly.

"Oh, no, you don't," Sophie said.

"Did you have a big wedding?" Katie asked, hesitantly moving a little closer to the horses. Benjy and Boomer were eyeing her through the fence, looking for some attention.

"It wasn't big, but it sure wasn't a courthouse thing. It was wonderful, intimate, just what we wanted. But this,

this calls for something opulent and extravagant." Sophie patted Galahad firmly on the neck. "You're making a statement and sending a message."

Sophie and Stone's moving ceremony on the waterfront had been a joy to attend. But their situation was completely different than mine and Joe's. It occurred to me that opulent and extravagant might cover up the lack of depth in our feelings.

"I agree," I said to Sophie. "Opulent and extravagant is the way to go."

"So, we can help you plan," Katie said, sounding even more enthusiastic.

"You're a sap as well as being a pragmatist?" I asked her.

Sophie gave Katie a conspiratorial look. "Joe's not going to care what we do so long as it hits the Alaskan news."

"Budget?" Katie asked Sophie, her brow rising.

Sophie gave a chopped laugh at that. "Xavier and Braxton will spring for a space shuttle flyby if we ask them."

"I know a couple of people at NASA," Katie said.

"No space shuttle," I insisted, knowing it was a joke but genuinely worried about how big these two might go.

Treat Yourself with 2 Free Books!

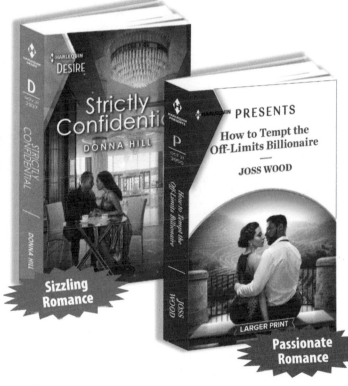

Sizzling Romance

Passionate Romance

GET UP TO 4 FREE BOOKS & 2 FREE GIFTS WORTH OVER $20

See Inside For Details

Claim Them While You Can

Get ready to relax and indulge with your **FREE BOOKS** and more!

Claim up to FOUR NEW BOOKS & TWO MYSTERY GIFTS – absolutely FREE!

Dear Reader,

We both know life can be difficult at times. That's why it's important to treat yourself so you can relax and recharge once in a while.

And I'd like to help you do this by sending you this amazing offer of up to FOUR brand new full length FREE BOOKS that WE pay for.

This is everything I have ready to send to you right now:

Try **Harlequin® Desire** books featuring the worlds of the American elite with juicy plot twists, delicious sensuality and intriguing scandal.

Try **Harlequin Presents® Larger-Print** books featuring the glamorous lives of royals and billionaires in a world of exotic locations, where passion knows no bounds.

Or **TRY BOTH!**

All we ask in return is that you answer 4 simple questions on the attached Treat Yourself survey. You'll get **Two Free Books** and **Two Mystery Gifts** from each series you try, *altogether worth over $20*! Who could pass up a deal like that?

Sincerely,

Pam Powers

Harlequin Reader Service

Treat Yourself to Free Books and Free Gifts.

Answer 4 fun questions and get rewarded.

We love to connect with our readers! Please tell us a little about you...

▶ **DETACH AND MAIL CARD TODAY!** ▶

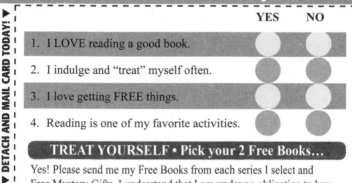

	YES	NO
1. I LOVE reading a good book.		
2. I indulge and "treat" myself often.		
3. I love getting FREE things.		
4. Reading is one of my favorite activities.		

TREAT YOURSELF • Pick your 2 Free Books...

Yes! Please send me my Free Books from each series I select and Free Mystery Gifts. I understand that I am under no obligation to buy anything, as explained on the back of this card.

Which do you prefer?

☐ **Harlequin Desire®** 225/326 HDL GRAN
☐ **Harlequin Presents® Larger-Print** 176/376 HDL GRAN
☐ **Try Both** 225/326 & 176/376 HDL GRAY

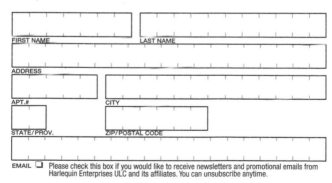

FIRST NAME _____ LAST NAME _____

ADDRESS _____

APT.# _____ CITY _____

STATE/PROV. _____ ZIP/POSTAL CODE _____

EMAIL ☐ Please check this box if you would like to receive newsletters and promotional emails from Harlequin Enterprises ULC and its affiliates. You can unsubscribe anytime.

© 2022 HARLEQUIN ENTERPRISES ULC
™ and ® are trademarks owned by Harlequin Enterprises ULC. Printec in the U.S.A.

Your Privacy – Your information is being collected by Harlequin Enterprises ULC, operating as Harlequin Reader Service. For a complete summary of the information we collect, how we use this information and to whom it is disclosed, please visit our privacy notice located at https://corporate.harlequin.com/privacy-notice. From time to time we may also exchange your personal information with reputable third parties. If you wish to opt out of this sharing of your personal information, please visit www.readerservice.com/consumerschoice or call 1-800-873-8635. **Notice to California Residents** – Under California law, you have specific rights to control and access your data. For more information on these rights and how to exercise them, visit https://corporate.harlequin.com/california-privacy.

HD/HP-520-TY22

◆ HARLEQUIN® Reader Service —**Here's how it works:**

Accepting your 2 free books and 2 free gifts (gifts valued at approximately $10.00 retail) places you under no obligation to buy anything. You may keep the books and gifts and return the shipping statement marked "cancel." If you do not cancel, approximately one month later we'll send you more books from the series you have chosen, and bill you at our low, subscribers-only discount price. Harlequin Presents® Larger-Print books consist of 6 books each month and cost $5.80 each in the U.S. or $5.99 each in Canada, a savings of at least 11% off the cover price. Harlequin Desire® books consist of 6 books each month and cost just $4.55 each in the U.S. or $5.24 each in Canada, a savings of at least 13% off the cover price. It's quite a bargain! Shipping and handling is just 50¢ per book in the U.S. and $1.25 per book in Canada.* You may return any shipment at our expense and cancel at any time — or you may continue to receive monthly shipments at our low, subscribers-only discount price plus shipping and handling. *Terms and prices subject to change without notice. Prices do not include sales taxes which will be charged (if applicable) based on your state or country of residence. Canadian residents will be charged applicable taxes. Offer not valid in Quebec. Books received may not be as shown. All orders subject to approval. Credit or debit balances in a customer's account(s) may be offset by any other outstanding balance owed by or to the customer. Please allow 3 to 4 weeks for delivery. Offer available while quantities last. **Your Privacy** — Your information is being collected by Harlequin Enterprises ULC, operating as Harlequin Reader Service. For a complete summary of the information we collect, how we use this information and to whom it is disclosed, please visit our privacy notice located at https://corporate.harlequin.com/privacy-notice. From time to time we may also exchange your personal information with reputable third parties. If you wish to opt out of this sharing of your personal information, please visit www.readerservice.com/consumerschoice or call 1-800-873-8635. **Notice to California Residents** — Under California law, you have specific rights to control and access your data. For more information on these rights and how to exercise them, visit https://corporate.harlequin.com/california-privacy.

▲ If offer card is missing write to: Harlequin Reader Service, P.O. Box 1341, Buffalo, NY 14240-8531 or visit www.ReaderService.com ▼

BUSINESS REPLY MAIL
FIRST-CLASS MAIL   PERMIT NO. 717   BUFFALO, NY

POSTAGE WILL BE PAID BY ADDRESSEE

HARLEQUIN READER SERVICE
PO BOX 1341
BUFFALO NY 14240-8571

NO POSTAGE
NECESSARY
IF MAILED
IN THE
UNITED STATES

Six

Sophie and Katie had gone big.

I hadn't paid much attention to the wedding planning, because my engagement to Joe had worked exactly as my dad and Braxton predicted. With the senator's support, the next round of funding for the arts and culture complex was approved, contracts were awarded and my on-site office was up and running.

The response from the community was gratifying. We'd hired a second architectural firm, plus engineers and construction companies. Volunteers were eager to stay involved, and we had several advisory committees set up from the arts community, the economic and tourism sectors, and from the city beautification board.

The plans included a performance theater, gallery and exhibition space, a convertible ballroom, classrooms, public spaces, and a top-floor restaurant overlooking the water. The exterior was designed in curves and angles, using natural materials and a color scheme that would blend with the mountains and the ocean.

Multilevel parking would be tucked away at the side of the building, screened by a narrow green space, while the prime outdoor area would be staged and landscaped for performances and festivals. My excitement built by the day, especially now that construction companies were on-site and we were getting ready to pour the foundation.

Sophie and Katie had taken the wedding planning completely off my shoulders. Katie had seen more of my family than me these past weeks. It freed up my time to focus on work and meant I didn't have to dwell on the fact I was marrying Joe. Other than wearing my engagement ring—a beautiful solitaire with a twisted band and diamond chips inset—not much had changed.

But that was going to end this weekend in Anchorage. Thursday was the final dress fitting. Since Sophie and I were the same size, she'd been the model for the dress, sending me pictures along the way. It was, in a word, spectacular—bright white with drop cap sleeves, a sweetheart neckline, a tight bodice with shimmering beaded lace flowing softly to layers of chiffon in the billowing ball gown skirt, then finished with matching beaded lace along the hem.

Then Friday was the rehearsal dinner, Saturday the ceremony, and I'd been told I was going on a honeymoon to Joe's family ranch on the Kenai Peninsula. They had a beautiful guesthouse on the shore of a small lake where we'd have privacy. I loved the Kenai Peninsula, so I looked forward to the mini vacation, even if I did feel like I was an actor participating in someone else's wedding.

Though I'd tried to slow them down, the days and the events flew by, and in what felt like moments, I was standing in front of the full-length mirror in the bathroom off my bedroom in the mansion, dressed in the gorgeous creation with Sophie's stylist Kari-Anne offering me the choice of a crystal hair comb, a spray of tiny white flowers or a veil.

"I'm not wild about the veil or the flowers," I told her. "Would the comb hold okay with my hair so short? I was thinking at the back."

Kari-Anne looked doubtful. "I can give it a try."

"Ask me now if I miss my hair," I said to Katie. I'd had the auburn roots lightened to match the new color. It had grown out some, but it was still very short.

"Your new hair is really pretty," Sophie said with a tone and enthusiasm obviously intended to placate an anxious bride.

"I was only joking," I assured her.

I wasn't a typical stressed-out bride, worried about having a perfect day. Quite the opposite. In an hour or so, I'd walk down the aisle in this very stately princess dress, with something bride-like on my head, say some temporary vows to Joe, spend a couple of days in woodsy luxury to make the package complete, then get back to my regular life.

"What do you suggest?" I asked Kari-Anne.

"How about this?" She pulled at the wires that held the crystals, straightening them and shaping the comb into a long, thin line. She anchored it a few inches back from my hairline.

It was a tiara look, which I would never have considered, but it was delicate and subtle against the light blond hair color.

"Oh, yeah," Sophie said as Kari-Anne stood back.

"That's awesome," Katie said.

Their bridesmaid dresses were twilight-blue chiffon with sweetheart necklines, off-the-shoulder straps and flowing skirts. Their bodices were snug, pleated with a front knot. We'd all gone with diamond earrings and pendant necklaces. They both looked terrific. You couldn't even tell Sophie was pregnant.

I smiled at the sight of us all in the mirror.

"We're gorgeous," Katie said.

"You two have done an amazing job," I said.

Sophie rubbed my arm. "You'll do great."

"I suppose you ordered me a big ol' bouquet."

They laughed and exchanged glances, telling me the flowers were going to be as extravagant as the dress.

"Wait till you see it," Sophie said and ducked out of the room.

Kari-Anne followed her.

As soon as they left, Katie's expression sobered. "You're sure about this, right?"

"Not in the least." My answer was flippant.

Who could be sure about something like this? But I was going for it anyway. All day long I'd kept a smile on my face and pushed reality out of my mind, knowing the wheels of fate were churning and I couldn't stop them if I tried.

Katie seemed to see past the facade. "Seriously, Adeline. You're *getting married.*"

"I know. I can tell by the outfit."

"Quit joking around."

"I can't." At this point I was afraid to stop joking.

"It's not too late to back out."

"No," I said firmly. "Well…maybe." Then I shook off the wayward thought. "I made this decision when I was calm and rational. I'm not changing it while I'm panicking."

"Panicking is not a good sign in a bride."

"All brides panic." At least, I thought they must panic,

because every wedding was a very big deal. For better or worse, you were hitching your life to someone else's.

My heart began to thump against my chest.

"Sophie?" Katie's tone sounded worried as Sophie came back into the bathroom, the big bouquet in her hand.

She took in our expressions. "What happened? What's going on?"

"You were a bride," Katie said to her. "Did you panic right before the ceremony?"

"No." Sophie looked confused.

Katie nodded her head at me. "Adeline's panicking."

"I'm fine," I said. I just needed to catch my breath.

"Adeline?" Sophie asked with concern, moving closer.

"Let me see the bouquet," I said in a hearty voice, holding out my hand while the room seemed to grow hot. My stomach knotted, and a funny buzzing sound came up in my ears.

"She's white as a ghost," Katie said.

I felt her hand on my arm.

"I'm getting Joe," Sophie announced.

"No!" I managed. I didn't want Joe to see me like this. I just needed a minute to gather my thoughts.

But Sophie left anyway.

"Sit down." Katie steered me to the little bench in front of my vanity counter. "Breathe."

I did. I focused on breathing, telling myself to buck up already, that this was just another step in the grand plan. I was playing a role, dressed in a costume. Joe would play his part. We'd smile, gaze at each other, pretend we were happy, and it would all be over before I knew it.

"Adeline?"

I lifted my gaze to see Joe walk in and Katie slip out of the bathroom.

He was dressed in a crisp, very formal black tux, a

white shirt and a silver tie. His hair was finely trimmed, and his face was perfectly shaven.

He crouched beside me. "What's going on?"

"Isn't this bad luck?" I managed.

"The bride passing out before the ceremony is bad luck."

"I'm not passing out."

"Sophie said you turned gray."

"I didn't turn gray."

He took my hand. Then he took my other hand, too. "You're freezing."

"We are in Alaska."

"It's July."

"I'm nervous," I admitted. "Aren't you nervous? There are… Do you know how many people are coming to the wedding?"

"I don't know. Maybe five hundred."

"That's a lot of people." I swallowed. "For us to lie to."

He lifted my hands to his lips and gave them a gentle kiss. "We're not lying to them."

"Misleading, misdirecting." A person could call it whatever they wanted.

"We really are getting married, Adeline."

"Does your family know the truth?" I wondered if we'd have to keep up the facade around his parents and his two sisters.

"They know you're pregnant. They know we weren't dating before it happened. They don't know the whole backstory like yours does, but they know this isn't exactly a normal marriage."

I searched his expression. "Are you having second thoughts?"

"Not a one."

"Why? How can you walk blithely into a sham marriage?"

"Is there a reason we didn't have this conversation before now?"

"No." The answer didn't sound right to my own ears. "I wasn't really thinking about it before." I looked down at myself. "This dress, the hair, the flowers."

"You look very beautiful."

"I look like bad luck."

He gave a half smile. "You know you're sounding a little emotional."

"I think maybe I am a little emotional." I was trying to think straight, but fear and uncertainty were clouding my mind.

He gently touched my chin with his index finger. His fingertip was warm. His gaze was warm. "We're going to be fine."

"You don't know that."

"I'm going to do everything in my power to make sure we're fine."

I believed him. "Do you generally succeed at things like that?"

"Mostly, yes."

"Well, I mostly fail." Today was the culmination of a cascading series of my failures in life.

"You don't have to change your life for this, Adeline." His gaze lowered to my still-flat stomach. "Well, you know. There is the baby."

He coaxed a smile from me.

"We'll take it one step at a time," he said. "I promise."

"Okay," I said with a little nod. "Okay."

He stood and held out his hand to me.

The knot in my stomach loosened a bit as I reached up to take his sturdy, warm hand. I then rose to my feet.

"You really do look amazing. I hope they take lots of pictures."

"Sophie hired three photographers."

"We can always count on Sophie." He searched my face. "You good?"

"I'm good." I was. At least I was better. The room temperature felt normal again, and the buzzing was gone from inside my ears. I took those as good signs.

I looked down at the oversize, elegant bouquet of cream and blush roses, cradled by succulent greenery and white jasmine, that was resting on the countertop. "You have to wonder what they're going to spring on us for a cake."

"None of that matters." Joe took my hand again and rubbed his thumb over my engagement ring.

"What matters to you?" I wanted to remind myself of why we were doing this.

"Our baby."

"Not your political career?"

"Sure. Your career matters to you, too."

I couldn't deny that. I removed my hand from his. "It does."

"Beauty of this marriage," he said, "is it helps everything."

"That's the beauty of it." I felt like my mind was clear again.

"See you in the church?" he asked.

"See you in the church."

I was relieved to have the vows over and done with. I'd stared at the middle of Joe's forehead the whole time I spoke. His kiss to seal the deal had been quick, and I was prepared for the tingle it left on my lips. I didn't feel married yet, but I expected that would take a little time.

We were through the well-wishes at the church, and the photos in the park were finished as well as the more formal ones taken in the glass room at the Cannery House Pavilion, where the reception was being held. Afterward, I was tired of smiling and putting a blissful light on in my eyes.

Sebastian had presided over a seven-course, sit-down dinner for five hundred people. On top of that, Sophie and Katie had outdone themselves with the cake. It was iced and decorated in pure white with hints of gold and a cluster of fresh Alaskan wildflowers curving partway around the base. It was accompanied by dozens and dozens of gold-dusted lemon buttercream cupcakes set out on multitiered china platters. A great idea, I thought, since cutting five hundred slices of cake would have taken forever.

Hands together on a gold-plated knife, Joe and I made the ceremonial cut.

A waiter was on standby to transfer the first slice to a plate for us.

"You ready?" Joe whispered, putting a small nibble on a fork for me.

I appreciated that he wasn't making a big messy production out of it.

I took the bite and raised the fork, then did the same for him.

He grinned in faux delight, clearly as aware as I was of being the center of attention. He gave me another quick kiss on the lips. This one tingled, too. I wondered if that sensation would ever go away. I also wondered if we'd even do any more kissing. After tonight our obligations would be over and there'd be no more reason for public displays of affection.

Conversation started up, humming through the room as the guests relaxed after dinner and a small army of waiters began distributing cake and cupcakes. Champagne was being offered table to table, and the bar was seeing a fair amount of traffic. People looked like they were having fun, and that made me happy.

Stone had moved along the head table to chat with Sophie, while Mason, Kyle and Katie stood in a conversational group with Joe's sister Elaine.

"Joe." A beautifully dressed young woman pulled up the chair next to Joe. She looked to be about thirty-five, with long black hair and lovely fine features. She was wearing a deep burgundy halter dress in a filmy fabric with an A-line asymmetrical hemline.

"Hi, Charmaine," Joe said. "Adeline, have you met Charmaine Tan? She's my media assistant."

"Nice to meet you, Charmaine." Since I hadn't read the guest list, I had no idea who'd been invited on Joe's side. It made sense he'd invite his political staff.

Charmaine grinned at both of us. "You're trending."

"Trending what?" Joe asked.

"Trending, trending." She held up her phone and waved it back and forth. "They love Adeline. I mean, *love* her."

Joe's hand wrapped around mine. "What's not to love?"

"You should read some of this," she said, holding out her phone with eager enthusiasm.

"Charmaine." Joe glanced meaningfully around. "You do realize we're in the middle of a wedding."

She gave a little chuckle. "Don't I know it. It's demographic gold—eighteen- to thirty-five-year-old women, who are romantics, followed closely by eighteen- to thirty-five-year-old men. Let's face it, Adeline, you're hot."

"Excuse me?" Joe said.

"Don't be naive," Charmaine admonished. She gestured up and down my dress. "I mean, come on."

"It's our wedding," Joe repeated. "Put your phone down and have some cake."

"Not on your life. Numbers like these don't come along every day."

"Are you live-posting our wedding?" I asked.

"Of course," she said, thumb scrolling along her screen. "You walking down the aisle—great bouquet, by the way, and the dress is to die for. The kiss, in the park, entering the reception."

Joe took the phone from her and gaped. "Did we plan this live social media event?"

"What do you mean?" she asked.

"I mean, did the office put together a formal media strategy for my wedding?"

"Not exactly. I'm an opportunist."

Joe didn't look happy. "You should have given Adeline a heads-up."

Charmaine seemed taken aback by the criticism. She looked at me. "You didn't expect people would post pictures? I'm not the only one doing it."

"You're not?" I shouldn't have been shocked, but I was certainly surprised.

"It's not just the official feed that's blowing up. You have a hashtag. Hashtag JoeAdelineBliss, all one word."

I looked blankly at Joe.

Neither of us seemed to know what to say.

"This is fantastic," Charmaine said, excitement and encouragement in her voice. "So, where are you going on your honeymoon?"

"Don't tell them," I quickly said. I didn't think anyone would go to the trouble of following us down the Kenai, but I never imagined my wedding would be livestreamed, either.

Charmaine looked affronted at that. "I won't disclose the information. I want to book a ticket and come along."

"On our *honeymoon*?" Joe asked incredulously.

My feelings echoed his, though not for the usual reasons. I was bringing along my laptop. I couldn't exactly correspond with the project team while I was on my honeymoon, but I had plenty of detail design work I could move forward on alone. I didn't want to have to pretend it was a regular honeymoon for the benefit of Charmaine or the internet public.

"We need to keep this going," Charmaine said. "It's not like I'm going to cramp your style. Just a few shots at dinner, or in a hot tub, or on a walk along a beach."

"No," Joe said, his voice firm.

I breathed a sigh of relief.

"Did you see this?" Katie arrived beside my shoulder, her phone in her hand. "You two are famous."

"I heard we have a hashtag," I answered.

"More than one."

"The public loves them," Charmaine said to Katie.

"I'm Katie." Katie reached across me to shake Charmaine's hand.

"Charmaine, Joe's media assistant."

"You must be loving this."

"I can't stop calculating the ad value."

Katie grinned at that. "Millions, I bet."

"Millions indeed."

"You're a mercenary," I said to Katie, craning my neck to more easily talk with her. "And Charmaine wants to come on our honeymoon."

"That's a great idea," Katie said.

I gave her a glare.

"What? Isn't positive publicity one of the—" She cut off the question and gave me a meaningful look.

She was right. We were trying to boost Joe's congressional soft power in Alaska.

"I like her," Charmaine said of Katie, her thumbs moving fast over her phone.

Mason came up behind Katie. "We're heading out to the patio bar," he told her. "You thirsty?"

She gave him a bright smile. "Sure. I'll come along. You good?" she asked me.

"You don't think I'll take care of her?" Joe asked.

"You better." She squeezed my shoulder goodbye.

"What do you think about Charmaine's suggestion?" Joe asked me. "About the honeymoon?"

"It wasn't what I planned." I wasn't keen on having an audience while we were meant to be having pretend stolen moments. It wasn't that I expected anything sexy to happen. More that I didn't want us to be forced to spend too much time together looking blissful. I was sure Joe would bring along some work as well.

"She can stay up in the main ranch house."

I knew that would keep her a couple of miles away from us. We'd still have plenty of privacy.

"Sure," I said, giving in for the greater good. Who was I to say no to this golden publicity opportunity?

"Should I check for cameras?" I asked Joe as the bellman left the honeymoon suite at the Blue Bowhead Hotel. We were overnighting in Anchorage, then Stone was flying us down the Kenai Peninsula to the ranch.

"Even Charmaine's not that tenacious," Joe said on a chuckle as the door swung shut behind the man.

"She seemed pretty tenacious to me." I'd changed from my wedding gown to a mottled gold sheath of a cocktail dress, and Charmaine had taken several shots of our formal departure in a limousine. Now, I was anxious to get out of my shoes and put my feet up on something soft.

The hotel suite was the finest in Anchorage—a sprawling living room of sofas and armchairs around a stone-decorated gas fireplace, a round glass dining table with upholstered chairs, a huge whirlpool tub in its own cedar-planked, plant-festooned room with a skylight and about a hundred candles. Through a double doorway, I could see the bedroom was massive, with a four-poster bed, a love seat and tall corner windows.

I took one of the sofas, kicked off my high-heeled shoes and stretched my legs across the opposite cushion. Then I leaned back and closed my eyes.

"You okay?" Joe asked.

"I'm glad it's over," I answered honestly. "My feet are killing me, and I think my smile is going to crack."

"You thirsty?"

I was. I started to rise.

"I'll get it," he said quickly, removing his tux jacket and draping it over a chair. "What do you want?"

"A big ol' lime margarita with a salted rim."

"So, fruit juice," he said, making his way around the breakfast bar to the kitchenette.

"Whatever they've got," I said. "So long as it's liquid."

He brought me back an orange juice and a bottle of water for himself.

"You don't have to go nonalcoholic for me," I said as I opened the little wide-mouthed glass bottle.

"I'm not." He sat down on the opposite sofa.

We both gazed at each other for a minute.

"So…" he said.

"So…" I said back.

"We seem to be married."

I gave a mock toast with my juice. "Mission accomplished." I paused. "I didn't expect the rest of the world to get quite so excited about it."

"Me neither."

"Did we do the right thing?"

"Yes," he answered without hesitation.

Then he rose and ambled over, stripping off his silver tie along the way, unbuttoning the collar of his shirt and flipping the switch that turned on the gas fireplace. He reached down and lifted my feet, sitting then setting them to rest on his lap. "Tell me what you're thinking."

I tried to put my feelings into words, buying time by taking another sip of juice. "I'm wondering what happened along the way."

"Along what way?"

"Growing up. I was always so sure, so confident I knew exactly what I wanted, or at least what I should try to accomplish and what I should avoid. Now this…*this*."

"Not part of your plan, I know."

"I always wanted independence. I didn't like being a Cambridge, didn't want expectations put on me, didn't want my life's path charted before I could even figure out what life was."

"If you know what life is, you're way ahead of everyone else."

"I felt like I was off to the right start in California, down there in school." I took another drink, pondering the shakeup of my girlhood vision and about to launch into another list of complaints. But then I realized I was becoming self-absorbed. "What about you?" I asked instead. "Did you grow up wanting to be in Congress?"

His features relaxed as he set his bottle of water on the side table. The light from the fireplace flames flickered against the planes of his face, and he wrapped a hand around one of my feet. "Can I?"

I startled a little from the unexpected touch. But he began massaging the arch, and I wanted to groan in pleasure.

"Sure," I said. What woman in the world would say no?

"This seems like a married kind of thing to do," he said with a quirky little smile as his fingers dug into my foot in an incredibly gratifying way. He massaged in silence for a moment. "I wanted to make a difference. No, that sounds too altruistic. I wanted to fix things. When I was in eleventh grade, we did a civics project on politics and decision making. It was the first time I thought about who made the rules of society and how those rules change people's lives, hopefully for the better, sometimes for the worse."

"Wanting to change people's lives still sounds very altruistic."

"I wanted things to work logically and reasonably."

"That doesn't sound much like politics to me."

"Turns out it's not." He switched to my other foot.

I had to stifle a groan again and started thinking maybe this married thing wasn't such a bad idea.

"There are intentions and agendas and backroom deals. And everybody needs to reapply for their job every two or four or six years, and they reapply to a very fickle group of voters. So that becomes the focus, unfortunately."

"You think you can do more as governor?"

"In some ways, yes. But I've got plenty of things I still want to do as a congress member."

"I assume Charmaine knows about the governor's run."

He nodded. "Charmaine has done this for a few years now. She's experienced enough to know how a public profile, especially a positive public profile, translates into leverage. She's doing her job."

"On *our* honeymoon." I wasn't sure why I said that. It wasn't like it was a real honeymoon. "I brought my laptop," I added. "I'm assuming you brought some work to do?"

"I know you can't ride horses, but I thought we'd go salmon fishing or whale watching. The charters off the island are world-class."

"You think we should fish?"

"Or we could go hiking if your feet aren't too sore."

I'd barely noticed, but his massage had moved to the back of my calf.

"You want us to spend our honeymoon together?" I asked, trying hard not to focus on the way his strong fingertips loosened my tight muscles.

"You didn't read the instruction manual for this, did you?"

"I guess with Charmaine coming along and everything, we will have to put on a show."

"Adeline." His hand stilled.

I fought my disappointment.

"I like you," he said.

I looked over and met his warm, coffee-dark gaze.

His eyes held mine captive as he switched to my other leg, moving this thumb into a knot just below my knee. "I just plain like you."

I held back a moan of pleasure. "So, you want to hang out."

"Yes. I want to hang out."

My mouth had gone dry, so I sipped some more juice.

His strokes became longer, touching the back of my knee, warming my skin with friction, sending shimmers of arousal along my thighs and higher still.

I felt myself slouching down, subconsciously easing closer to him, my silky dress riding up, giving him easy access to my bare thighs.

He feathered his fingertips across my goose-bumped skin.

I bit down on my bottom lip, my eyelids dropping closed. I let the desire pass through me, heating my belly, prickling my skin.

"Adeline?" His voice was husky deep.

"Yes?" Mine was breathless.

His hand smoothed higher still, caressing the inside of my thigh.

I sucked in a gasp of anticipation, my body tightening around itself.

But he stoked back down again, to my knee, my calf, my ankle.

I regretted it instantly. "Adeline?" he asked again.

"Yes?"

His hand made its way up.

I squirmed, and he stilled.

I grasped his hand, pulling it higher.

He tugged me his way, sliding my backside over the sofa, sending my skirt to my waist, baring the lacy white panties that had gone with my wedding dress.

He touched their high-cut border.

I watched as he ran his fingertip along the lace, dipping below it, following the curve of my hip, downward, downward.

"Adeline?" His voice rumbled through me.

"Yes?" I didn't expect an answer, but this time he gave me one.

"You maybe want to go have a wedding night?"

I lazily opened my eyes. I didn't want to move an inch. I wanted him to keep doing exactly what he was doing.

There was a dare in his expression—a tease and a dare—and he moved his fingertip another inch.

I stifled a gasp of pleasure. "You mean with sex and everything?"

He leaned down and put a row of featherlight kisses along my thigh. "With sex and everything."

"Oh, yes," I said, and he scooped me into his arms.

I lay back, stretching naked on the cool, smooth sheets of the luxurious bed, and Joe followed me down, smoothing my hair away from my face.

"You are the most beautiful vision I have ever seen," he whispered.

"Don't tell Sophie and Katie."

He gave me a puzzled smile. "Why not?"

"They had me in a fifty-thousand-dollar dress earlier."

"This is better." He stroked a hand lazily over my shoulder, dipping between my breasts.

"Plus a tiara," I said, my breathing speeding up.

His palm moved lower, settling on my stomach, stopping there, cradling me below my navel.

I cast my gaze down. "There's nothing to feel yet." I'd been checking every day, but my stomach hadn't changed a bit.

"The waiting only makes it sweeter," he said, then removed his hand and leaned down to kiss me there.

My heart fluttered and my chest tightened with wayward emotion.

He kissed me again and again, moving across my navel, higher and higher, spreading hot kisses that left cool, damp traces behind.

Desire coiled inside me. I reached out to him, smoothing my hands over his bare shoulders, reveling in his naked, solid strength.

He slowly shifted above me, over me, settling in the vee between my legs. His gaze fixed on mine as he lowered his lips, capturing my mouth, kissing me deeply, enfolding me in his arms.

The power of his kisses flowed through me. I inhaled the fresh scent of his hair, molding myself against him, wrapping my body around him, savoring every touch, every taste, every scent, anticipating the glorious moment we'd become one.

My hips reflexively arched, but I could feel his hesitation. "I don't want to hurt—"

"You won't," I said, pulling him to me.

"Tell me if—"

"You won't," I repeated.

I kissed him deeply, and his moan vibrated against my lips.

As he pressed inside, his hands began to roam. Desire overtook my senses. Our rhythm increased, sweat slickening our bodies, and passion lifted us higher and higher.

I cried out his name as the crescendo engulfed me.

He groaned and shuddered, his weight coming down to press me into the soft bed.

"Adeline," he whispered in my ear, his fingers tangling in my hairline. He kissed my swollen lips. Then he kissed them again.

He slowly rolled to his back, bringing me on top of him.

I lifted my head to focus.

His chest moving up and down, he tucked my hair behind my ears. "Do you still think we're scratching an itch?" He parroted my earlier words.

"I feel pretty scratched."

His expression faltered.

"In a good way," I quickly added, resting my head on his shoulder. "In a very good way."

He was silent for a while, our breathing gradually slowing in the silent room.

His hands were light on my bare back. His heart beat against mine as I rose and fell with his breaths.

"Did you eat at the wedding?" he asked in a soft voice.

"Not much," I said. I glanced at the bedside clock. It was well after midnight.

"I'm starving," he said. "How about you?"

"Hungry." I was hungrier than usual these days, that was for sure.

"Pizza and milkshakes?"

"I'm in. Can we get Hawaiian?"

"Anything you want." He gave me a kiss on the hairline. "But you have to move so I can call down."

While Joe made the call, I wrapped myself in a hotel robe and wandered back into the living room. I looked at my phone and saw my messages were stacking up. Friends and acquaintances, some people I'd barely met in college and high school, plus a huge number of students from classes where I'd been a teaching assistant, were all writing to congratulate me on getting married.

Curling up in an armchair, I scrolled through, skimming most of the messages as more arrived. I switched to email and found the same thing. I would have bet that I didn't even know this many people. And I didn't. But for some reason they all felt like they knew me.

"Something wrong?" Joe asked as he joined me, wrapped like I was in a fluffy white robe.

"There are hundreds of them," I said, reading as I scrolled: congratulations, best wishes, I'd love to call you, I'd love to hear from you and I'd love to make you a job offer. "This is wild."

He came around beside me.

"Emails, texts." I held up my phone so he could see. "It's not just social media chatter. I'm getting job offers."

"Anything good?" he asked with a little smile. He didn't seem to think it unusual.

"Nothing specific. Do you get this sort of thing all the time?"

"Not that many messages, not all at once." He moved to the twin chair next to mine and sat down.

"Check yours," I said.

He reached for his phone and brought up a screen.

"What are people saying to you?" I asked him.

"That I'm a lucky man."

I rolled my eyes in his direction. "No, seriously."

"Lots of congratulations, compliments to you, your dress—"

"It was a great dress."

"Asking for media interviews." He scrolled a little farther. "Uh, no."

"Uh, no what?"

"No, I'm not doing an interview on my honeymoon."

"Not even with Charmaine."

"Charmaine won't ask questions. She'll just take pictures. Here's one from her."

"Charmaine is writing to you at one thirty in the morning?" And I thought I had a dedicated team.

"She sent it earlier." He kept reading.

"Is it important?" It must be important. Charmaine would know what was important and what wasn't. I liked her from the start.

"There's a thing," he said.

"A bad thing?" I asked.

"A work thing." He seemed to hesitate. "There's a retreat near Charleston, South Carolina, the Select Committee on Regulatory Reform."

"That sounds fun." The sarcasm in my tone was pretty clear.

A knock on the suite door interrupted my joke.

"You'd be surprised," Joe said as he went to answer.

A waiter wheeled in a large, silver-covered platter and two tall vanilla milkshakes decorated with whipped cream.

The aroma was enticing, and my stomach gently rumbled in appreciation as Joe tipped the man and sent him on his way.

Not standing on ceremony, I rose and removed the silver cover and helped myself to one of the milkshakes. The aromas of ham, pineapple, cheese and the tender-looking crust were enticing.

Joe separated the plates from the cloth napkins and silverware. "You'd be surprised."

"About?" As far as I could see, we had exactly what we'd ordered. Using a serving knife, I transferred a slice of pizza to my plate.

"The Committee on Regulatory Reform."

"I don't think it would surprise me."

"It is exciting. At least I think it's exciting. Or maybe *satisfying* is the right word. Their work will change how all the other committees are managed going forward. We have the power to streamline everything from the passage of bills to the allocation of money to emergency response."

I sat back down in the armchair with my pizza. "I'm not really feeling the excitement."

He set his pizza and milkshake down on the coffee table, freeing his hands, clearly intending to use them to further illustrate his points. "How about this?"

I took a bite and settled in.

"It's a social occasion as well. Meetings during the day, but a pool, a beach, cocktails, a little sightseeing and dinner."

"That helps, I guess," I didn't know why he cared what I thought. I wasn't going to any great lengths to convince him that moving the theater ten degrees east was a stronger choice for the building silhouette for the arts and culture center.

"Charmaine thinks you should come."

I swallowed. "What?"

"I've received congratulations from every member of the committee. They all want to meet you. Charleston would be the perfect opportunity. It's not for two weeks."

My heart sank just a little. "I have work."

Joe nodded. "I know."

"I can't just up and leave the team for beachside cocktails in Charleston." I would have hoped he'd already understand that.

"It's only a couple of days."

"Plus travel time, that's four days. That's the better part of a week." I resented having to justify it.

He picked up his pizza and nodded, but I could see the disappointment in his expression.

"Joe."

"It's fine," he said.

"It can't be like this."

He looked my way. "Like what?"

"Like we're a traditional married couple—like I'm a political spouse who drops everything to attend functions with you."

It took him a minute to answer. "Nobody suggested you were that."

But he just had.

Seven

The honeymoon went off without a hitch. Charmaine respected our privacy but got several great publicity shots—the two of us enjoying a romantic balcony dinner, dancing under the midnight sun, and Joe on horseback, looking like a sexy rugged cowboy, with me perched on the corral fence watching. He'd gone out on a ride with his father then, giving me some time alone to dive into my work.

We tiptoed around each other for the most part. He didn't press me on coming to DC, and we didn't make love again. I was glad about both those things. After the unexpected wedding night, I felt like the honeymoon had set the right tone for our marriage.

Afterward, Joe stayed busy in Congress, while I pushed forward on the arts and cultural complex. We'd agreed to announce my pregnancy at three months. The calendar had clicked over, and I was beginning to wonder when the baby would start showing. I'd shared my curiosity with my doctor, and she'd told me I'd be growing out of my clothes soon enough and not to wish my trim waist away.

I was in the trailer office at the job site today, dressed in blue jeans and a navy cotton shirt over a pink tank top with a pair of steel-toed boots. My hair was getting back to its normal color and long enough now to be pulled back in a ponytail. I had a high-vis vest and an orange hard hat hanging on the wall in case I was needed out on the job site.

With the construction plans finished and finally approved, we'd doubled up on the crew size to get the foundation poured and the framing done before winter closed in on us. Concrete trucks came and went along the access road outside. Generators hummed, and clanking echoed from the two cranes setting up on the far side of the site. The days were still plenty long, so we had two full shifts, making the job roll out even faster.

My phone rang—a DC number, but not Joe or anyone in my contact list. I felt a brief shot of concern and quickly picked up. "Hello?"

"Adeline?" It was a woman's voice, one I vaguely recognized.

"It's me," I answered.

"It's Charmaine from Congressman Breckenridge's— I mean, Joe's office. Sorry, habit. I hope I haven't caught you at a bad time."

"No, it's fine. Is everything okay?"

"Good. Yes, all good here. I'm about to shoot you our official announcement on the baby. Congratulations, by the way. Joe wanted me to run it past you before we posted it. The photo is from the honeymoon, that late shot on the wharf in front of the lake. I really like the silhouettes and orange clouds in the background. Do you mind taking a look?"

"Sure. No problem." It was hard not to appreciate Joe's consideration in asking for my final approval.

"Great. Sent. You should get it any second." She paused. "While I've got you on the line…"

I could hear the hesitation in her voice. "Yes?"

"I know you weren't available for the Charleston event, and I understand. Joe's told us all how busy you are on the construction project. But I wondered if next Saturday might be even a remote possibility for you? It's the regulatory reform committee again. They're hosting a who's who mix-and-mingle event. Joe probably mentioned it already—the rumblings of offering him the chair?"

"Yes. Of course." I was bluffing. I had no idea what she meant.

"I probably don't have to tell you that he'd be the first Alaskan, the first Westerner and the youngest member to actually chair that committee. It's a pretty huge deal."

Joe hadn't said anything to me about becoming chair of anything. Then again, he didn't talk much about his job. We didn't talk all that much about anything, really, except to confirm all was well with the pregnancy.

"I know he ignores gossip," Charmaine continued. "And you probably do, too."

"Gossip?" I asked.

"Oh, nothing new. Just…you know…the stuff about you being in Alaska all the time and him being here. The baby announcement will—"

"Who's gossiping?" I couldn't help but ask.

"Nobody important."

Gerard, the head engineer, opened the office door, letting in the construction noise.

I gave him a five-minute hand signal, so he nodded and left.

"What's that?" Charmaine asked, obviously hearing the noise.

"Mostly diesel engines. I'm at the job site."

"Oh, I *am* disturbing you."

"What's the gist of it?" I asked. "The gossip, I mean. The latest," I added so she wouldn't guess that I didn't have the slightest knowledge of any news.

"Same old, same old—what does it mean that they spend so little time together. I *know* you're both busy, and that's our stock answer, but—" She stopped abruptly, seeming to think better of continuing.

"Go ahead," I said. "Please."

"You know what people are like, especially in this town, always looking to stir up trouble, especially the congressman's enemies."

"Joe has enemies?"

"*Everyone* in DC has enemies. Mostly people who are jealous. Every little notch of success and you pick up hundreds more. It's the way it works, the way it's always worked."

Listening, I couldn't help but feel guilty. I didn't intend to be a prop in Joe's political life, but I didn't want to cause him harm, either. The marriage had worked out well for my career so far, bringing the senator on board as my dad and uncle had predicted and catapulting our fund-raising efforts beyond our wildest hopes. It seemed like Joe deserved to get something out of it, too.

"Would it help if I came to the event on Saturday?" I was guessing that was why she'd asked.

I assumed attending the event would involve hanging on his arm, gazing adoringly into his eyes and laughing at every one of his jokes. Not that I ever had trouble laughing at Joe's jokes. He had a great sense of humor.

"Enormously. Could you do it?"

"I can try." I wasn't certain I could get away. It would be a stretch.

"Joe will be thrilled," she said.

"Can you hold off on telling him?"

My words were met with silence.

"Let's wait to see if I can get the time off. I don't want to make him a promise I can't keep."

At the very last minute, I'd managed to get away. There wasn't time to book a private jet, so I'd rushed to catch a red-eye out of Anchorage, thinking I'd call Joe in the air. But we were delayed taking off, then the in-flight Wi-Fi was malfunctioning.

Although my seat fully reclined, anticipation of seeing Joe had kept me awake. A dozen scenarios ran through my mind—him surprised, happy, annoyed, aloof. I didn't sleep at all on the plane.

When we finally landed at Ronald Reagan, my luggage was missing. And by the time I'd filled out all the forms in the wee hours of the morning, I was a zombie. I grabbed myself a hotel room near the airport and crashed for the next eight hours. Then I awoke to a dead phone battery with the charger packed away in my lost luggage.

The dead address book was down the list of my immediate worries. Time was running out, and without my suitcase, I needed to buy myself a new dress, pick up something in the way of formal jewelry, plus find a good cosmetologist who could work fast, since my makeup bag was missing along with everything else. On the upside, I'd ended up in a very service-oriented hotel, and the staff stepped up to help me with everything, including a rack of lovely dresses from the shop for me to choose from.

A stylist at the hotel's salon took one look at my part-blond, part-auburn hair and declared it a disaster area. When he found out I was attending a congressional event, he called over two assistants and they worked a miracle, matching the auburn tone and adding volume to create a pretty updo.

With my makeup professionally applied and me running only fifteen minutes late, with a still-dead phone in my new evening bag, the limo stopped in front of the event ballroom. The driver insisted on escorting me to the door.

"Your name, please, ma'am?" the doorman asked, tablet in his hand.

"Adeline Cambridge," I answered, trying unsuccessfully to peer at his list. "But I might not be on your—"

"Do you have an invitation, ma'am?"

"I'm a plus-one." I guessed that was the simplest way to put it.

"I'm afraid guests are also required to be preregistered. It's for security reasons."

I was impressed that the limo driver stood by waiting while I tried to talk my way in.

"Is there someone I can speak to?" I asked. "Maybe a manager who could vouch for—"

"We're not able to make exceptions, I'm afraid."

Another security guard moved to stand beside the first, likely because he was curious about the line forming behind me.

"Can I help with something?" the second man asked.

"Sir, I'm afraid Ms. Cambridge is not on the list."

The new, apparently higher-ranking security guard looked me over.

I couldn't imagine there was anything to make him suspicious. I knew I looked good all dressed up, exactly like the kind of guest they would expect at the high-end event. Still, his brow furrowed, like he thought my dress might be a knockoff or something.

"Is it possible to call Charmaine Tan?" I asked, thinking there had to be a straightforward way to clear this up. "She works for Congressman Breckenridge."

"All guests are required to have prior security clearance," he repeated.

I didn't want to do it, but I could see I had no choice. "What about Congressman Breckenridge? Could he clear me to come in?"

The man's lips thinned now. Clearly, he wasn't about to bother a congressman over a woman he thought was trying to crash the party.

I leaned in closer, and both men tensed, obviously ready for anything.

But all I wanted to do was lower my voice. "I'm *Mrs.* Congressman Breckenridge."

The first man paused at that. They looked at each other, obviously gauging my honesty.

"It has to be pretty easy to prove one way or the other," I offered.

"Wait right here, ma'am," the higher-ranking one said.

"Can you step to one side?" the original guard asked me, though his tone was more polite now. He obviously thought there was at least an outside chance I was who I said I was.

"Of course." I didn't want to hold anyone else up.

The driver moved with me.

"Thanks for waiting," I told him.

"Not a problem. I'm guessing you really are her."

"I am."

"You mind if I tell this story back at the garage?"

"Sure." I gave him a grin. I couldn't see the harm. Everyone had only been doing their jobs, and quite professionally.

A few minutes later, Joe appeared, walking at a brisk pace. He spotted me and practically elbowed his way past the security guard.

"Adeline?" He was clearly shocked to see me there.

I was surprised Charmaine had kept quiet all the way to now, not that I'd confirmed I was coming. Up to the last minute, I'd thought I wouldn't make it.

"Happy ending," the driver muttered to me in an undertone.

"Thanks for your help," I told him.

"Enjoy your evening." He stepped back.

Joe pulled me into a hug, and a few cameras flashed in my peripheral vision. I realized I was going to have to get used to that.

Aware of the people around us, I gave him a brilliant smile. "Sorry I'm late, darling. There was a flight delay out of Anchorage." I expected that sounded reasonable for anyone overhearing.

"No problem," he said, also smiling for the cameras as he put an arm around my waist and guided me toward the entrance.

Nobody stopped us this time, and in minutes we were in a calm entry hall outside the main ballroom.

"Why didn't you *call* me?" he asked.

"Some things went wrong. Lots of things went wrong."

"How did you know to come here?"

"Charmaine. I didn't think I could make it, so we didn't say anything to you. And then the flight was late, and I was desperate to sleep, but my phone died, and they lost my luggage, so I couldn't recharge the thing. And, wow, making up for lost luggage takes a lot of time."

"Charmaine *knew*?" There was frustration in his tone as we passed a few curious-looking people.

"Look happy," I warned him, looking happy myself.

His brow furrowed, and he gave a little shake of his head.

"The gossip. Look happy. We're blissfully newlywed, remember?"

My words seemed to penetrate, because he quickly smoothed out his expression and put on a smile.

An older couple spotted him and diverted across the lobby to approach us. "Congratulations on the baby, Breckenridge." The gray-haired man heartily shook Joe's hand.

"Thank you, Mr. Renfrew."

"Call me Seth. Call me Seth."

"Thank you, Seth. This is my wife, Adeline."

Mrs. Renfrew stepped closer to me. "I recognize you from your pictures. Congratulations, dear." The older woman was neatly coiffed and beautifully dressed in flowing black silk.

"Thank you, ma'am."

"Please, call me Maisie. I've been wanting to meet you since the wedding."

"The Renfrews are major patrons of the Bernadette Theater Organization," Joe said.

"That's a very worthy cause," I said, knowing a little bit about the work the organization did with youth performers.

"We have six children of our own," she said.

My eyes went wide. "Six?"

"And seven grandchildren," Seth added.

"We got a little carried away," Maisie said to me. Her tone turned conspiratorial, and she leaned in close. "Optimally, I'd recommend two, maybe three."

"I think I'll take your advice," I said back.

"It was great to see you both," Joe said to them, shaking Seth's hand one more time. "Please, enjoy the evening."

I could see out of the corner of my eye another couple waiting to talk to Joe. They were younger and expressed the same congratulations on the baby, and Joe told me they were involved in grizzly bear habitat remediation. The woman was excited to learn I'd once encountered a grizzly in the wild.

They were followed by a group of five, then another couple, then a young man on his own. I started to lose track as we slowly inched our way toward the ballroom.

"Is it always like this?" I asked Joe when we finally made it through a set of double doors. My jaw was already sore from smiling and talking.

"That was more attention than usual," he said, drawing back to take in my outfit. It was a full-length champagne satin dress, strapless with a straight neckline and a beaded bodice, dangling crystal earrings, and a matching necklace, and new, twinkling, barely there heeled sandals that I'd decided I loved.

"Your hair looks fantastic," he said.

"They added some volume." I gingerly touched the back of my neck. I couldn't take credit for growing out that much in only a few weeks.

I looked around the elaborately decorated ballroom festooned with white linen tablecloths and chair coverings, fine crystal, tall fresh flower centerpieces, and a beautifully draped stage. I saw gazes begin stopping on us. For a moment I felt like a bride again, the center of attention. Then I felt like a gazelle on the Serengeti as a few people eased their way closer, casually, like they didn't want to spook us.

I moved closer to Joe and took his hand. "They're all staring," I mumbled.

"They're looking at you."

"That's what makes me nervous."

He tipped his head close to talk privately. "Nervous? Are you kidding? I just heard you stared down a grizzly."

"My brothers were with me. Mason had a twelve-gauge."

He gave my hand a little squeeze. "Well, now you have me."

"Are you armed?"

"Only with my wit and charm. Hello, Judge Palomino."

The chitchat and introductions started all over again until we finally made it to our assigned table with three other congress members, one man and two women, along with their spouses.

"You made it," Charmaine whispered in my ear from behind, her hand coming down on my shoulder.

Joe turned and gave her a look that said he was displeased.

Charmaine caught the look, and her expression faltered before she turned her attention back to me. "I've been calling and calling."

"I'm sorry," I told her. "My phone died last night, and the charger is lost somewhere in the bowels of the airline's luggage storage. Or maybe it's on its way to London by now. I didn't have your number, and I had to buy a new dress and—"

"It's *not* a problem," Charmaine quickly said.

"And I was the last to know because…?" Joe asked, his voice low as well.

"That was my fault," I said.

Joe looked back and forth between us. "So that's how it's going to be?"

"It's not going to be anything," I said. "I asked her not to tell you because I didn't think I'd make it. Simple as that."

"You're blowing up the internet again," Charmaine said, clearly not seriously bothered by Joe's criticism. She held out her phone for us to look.

"Can you charge Adeline's phone?" Joe asked Charmaine.

"Right away."

"Can you do that here?" I asked her.

"The hotel will have charging stations in their business center. I'll take care of it. I'm hearing from the Sunday shows," she said to Joe as I gratefully got out my phone.

"Local?" he asked.

"Yes, but also New York."

"The big ones?"

"Simone Sackett wants you on live. Nothing hard-hitting, just a human angle."

I handed Charmaine my phone. "That's a good thing, right?" I knew the Simone Sackett show. It was highly popular, carried nationally on Sunday mornings and often excerpted later by the networks.

"What do you think?" Joe asked me.

"Whatever you want." I didn't see that it had much to do with me.

"So, you'll *do* it?" Charmaine asked me.

I took in their surprised expressions. "What, *me*?"

"Both of you," she said. "Oh, wow, she'll be my best friend all month."

"Wait," I said sharply, then realized I'd attracted attention from the others at the table. I lowered my voice. "I thought you meant Joe."

"Nobody wants to book me on a Sunday show," he said.

"You're the draw," Charmaine told me. "It'll be easy, straightforward everyday things, like *when's the baby due?*" She took in my stricken expression. "If you want to be vague about it, you say something along the lines of *late spring*, or *early summer*, and then you pivot by saying, *and we're really excited to decorate the nursery.* I guarantee you the next question will be about the nursery."

"I—" The idea of live television was beyond daunting.

"If you get really stuck, you can always change the subject entirely by saying something like, *the important thing to remember is thousands of children benefit across the nation from the new preschool program.*"

I couldn't see myself doing that.

Joe took my hands in his. "How about this? If you get

stuck on anything, anything at all, just touch your nose and tuck your hair behind your ear."

I couldn't help but smile, remembering it had been my signal at breakfast with Braxton and my father.

"That'll be his signal," Charmaine said.

"I'll start talking and you won't have to say a word." Joe's words were reassuring.

"Do you want this?" I asked him. I was still feeling like I'd benefited more than him from our partnership.

"*Yes,*" Charmaine said eagerly.

"Only if you're comfortable," Joe said.

"Okay," I said, taking a bracing breath. I could be the good wife for another day.

Charmaine had somehow magically sent three different outfits to Joe's condo, all in my size. But it was near midnight when we arrived, so I decided I'd figure out what to wear in the morning.

"This is really nice," I said, taking in his long living and dining room, the view through the kitchen doorway and the stairway the went up from the entryway to the second floor.

He paused next to a big corner sofa and two matching armchairs that faced a brick fireplace. "You can't be all that impressed. I've seen your house."

"That's not my house. It's my family's house."

"Yours as much as theirs." An odd expression crossed his face. "You think maybe we should have written a pre-nup?"

It was the first I'd thought of it, but I had a hard time taking the idea seriously. "Why? Are you after my house?"

"So, *now* it's your house?"

"A court might see it as partly mine. You know, for the purposes of your settlement." I strode a little way into the room and ran my fingertips across a marble sculpture. "You've got some pretty nice stuff here yourself, Congressman Breckenridge."

"Shopping?" he asked.

"Maybe."

"Your family's worth quite a bit more than mine."

I gave a shrug. "Maybe. But I could use a few Black Angus cattle."

He smiled at that. "Why didn't you ask for a prenup?"

"Why didn't you? Seriously, Joe, if things didn't end well, you don't think Xavier and Braxton would take you down?"

Joe chuckled. "They would." He let the subject drop and glanced at the stairs. "I've got a guest room up there. It's my office, but if I move a few things, I can pull out the sofa bed for myself."

That sounded complicated and time-consuming, especially considering we had a morning flight to Manhattan. "What time do we have to get up?"

"Five should do it."

"Let's just crash in your bed." It wasn't like we'd never shared one before.

"You okay with that?"

"We are married."

He gave a roguish grin. "We are."

"I meant for sleeping," I said. *"Sleeping."*

"Upstairs." He pointed. "First door at the top. En suite's all yours. I can use the bathroom at the end of the hall."

Talking about bed made me realize I was really tired. I started for the stairs, and he followed me up.

"Do you have some pajamas I can borrow?" I asked as we entered his spacious bedroom. "Just the top would work."

He paused. "I was, uh, going to go with boxers."

"You don't own pajamas?"

He shook his head. "Shirt? T-shirt, dress shirt? Help yourself to whatever you want." He gestured to a wide walnut dresser and a walk-in closet door.

He left me to it, and I hesitated, feeling like I was invading his privacy, but curious all the same. Like the rest of the condo, his bedroom was nicely laid out, with a king-size bed and two small armchairs set out in a bay window. It was done in grays and blues with a pale wood parquet flooring and a large, framed oil painting of his ranch house above the bed.

I'd really liked it on the Breckenridge ranch, and I wondered if I'd ever get a chance to go back. I hadn't wanted to ride a horse while I was newly pregnant, but I liked riding, and the Kenai Peninsula was one of the most ruggedly beautiful places on earth. I could picture the two of us on a cliff-side trail overlooking the waves of the ocean.

It would be three of us by then, I realized. I put my hand on my flat stomach and tried to imagine it growing round. It felt a little harder than usual, but otherwise, there was no change. I told myself to take my doctor's advice and stop feeling impatient.

I hesitated over opening Joe's dresser drawers. I didn't know what I expected to find, but I couldn't bring myself to rummage around in them.

I went to the closet instead, finding a row of pressed shirts, mostly white. I helped myself to one then headed for the en suite bathroom, closing the door behind me. Alongside his shaving kit I found liquid soap and a stack of fresh washcloths. Towels were stacked beneath the counter, with two big bath sheets hanging next to a walk-in shower.

After washing my face and removing my contacts, I went to work on my hair, pulling out the fasteners and combing it free. It felt very good to shake it loose. It also felt good to step out of my shoes. They were beautiful but hard on the feet by the end of the evening. I stripped down and buttoned myself into Joe's shirt. It smelled faintly of his earthy soap brand, and I held the fabric to my nose for a moment. Then I rolled up the sleeves, put my glasses on, folded my clothes into a stack and carried them back into the bedroom.

Joe was sitting up in the bed, chest bare, covers at his waist, his tablet on his lap. The shadow of his beard looked sexy across his square chin in the soft lamplight. He watched me walk to the opposite side of the bed. "You sure don't make this easy, Mrs. Breckenridge."

"Mrs. Breckenridge?" I asked on a laugh as I lifted the corner of the covers.

His tone was husky. "The very sexy Mrs. Breckenridge."

"Oh, no, you don't," I said, tempting though it was to slide into his arms—unnervingly tempting. "We have about five hours before your alarm goes off. You did set an alarm, right?"

"All set," he said as I swung my legs under the covers. "They might call you Mrs. Breckenridge tomorrow. Will it bother you?"

"I'll be more bothered by invasive questions about my personal life." I got settled on the comfortable bed and smoothed the covers. Deciding two pillows were too many, I tossed one onto an armchair.

"Do you think we should get our stories straight?" he asked.

"I was planning to stick to the truth. Well, except for the pregnancy timing. That's nobody else's business."

"How did we meet?" he asked.

I turned my head to look at him, gauging if he was joking. It didn't look like he was joking.

"The Kodiak Communications family picnic," I said.

He looked puzzled. "We did?"

"I was eleven, and you were heading off to Harvard. You won the obstacle course *and* the one-mile run. Mason was ticked off. He said it wasn't fair that you were so smart and so athletic."

"You were just a kid."

"I remember thinking you were funny. You did a back-flip at the end of the obstacle course and still had the fast-est time."

"Sounds like I was a show-off and you were in braces. We have to come up with a better story than that."

I smiled, because I *had* worn braces back then. "When do you remember us first meeting?"

"In your backyard, the first Saturday evening in June after your first year at Cal State, somewhere around eight o'clock. I was senior adviser to Governor Walmsley and try-ing to get your uncle's support for his reelection. You were tanned, wearing faded cutoffs, a cropped white T-shirt and a pair of white canvas sneakers, and I was thinking your dad should have had me arrested for where my mind was going."

I gave a little laugh, thinking it had to be a joke. He couldn't possibly remember what I'd been wearing one summer eight years ago.

"I was drinking twenty-one-year-old McIsaac when Braxton called you over and introduced you."

"I don't remember." I'd met a lot of people in suits dur-ing those years, many coming by the house to talk busi-ness with my dad and Braxton.

"That's okay. I wasn't trying to make an impression. I was trying to keep my hormones under control. You were gorgeous then...still are." His gaze took in my makeshift nightgown and heated in a way that I recognized. "And you look way too good in my shirt."

I swallowed, dampening down my own hormones. "Are we going with that, then?"

"That I lusted after you when you were nineteen? I don't think so."

"How about you were a longtime friend of the family, and neither of us remembers the exact moment we met, but it was likely at a business event in Anchorage?"

"Boring," he said.

"You want to come up with an interesting lie? I think we're better off sticking as close as we can to the truth. You know, within reason. Vague, like Charmaine suggested."

"Let's say we met at a Kodiak Communications corporate function and pretend we remember which one."

"Are you sure we should be winging this?" Now I was worried we hadn't planned enough in advance.

A live television interview seemed overwhelming at the moment. I stifled a yawn. Then again, the pregnancy had me more tired than usual. Maybe I only needed some sleep.

He smiled sympathetically. "We'll be fine. Just remember—" He tucked my hair behind my ear. "The secret signal."

"I will." That much I could do. I took off my glasses and snuggled down under the covers, determined to get some sleep. I'd do a whole lot better tomorrow if my brain wasn't sleep-deprived.

What felt like ten seconds later, Joe's alarm was chiming, waking me out of a toasty, warm sleep.

I shifted and instantly realized his arms were wrapped around me. My back was pressed snugly against him, his face burrowed in the crook of my neck, trapping my hair.

He inhaled. "Morning."

"Uh…" I wasn't exactly embarrassed—well, embarrassed to like it so much, and embarrassed to want to turn in his arms and to kiss him and see where that led.

But he pulled away before I could do anything. "You want breakfast? Coffee before we head to the airport?"

"A shower," I said, pulling myself together. If I was going to be on live television, my priority was a wake-up shower and a hair wash.

Simone Sacket's questions started off easily enough, where we'd each grown up and thoughts about Alaska.

Then, sure enough, she asked how we'd met.

Joe took the question, smoothly answering what we'd discussed about a corporate function.

But then she turned to me.

"How did that work later?" Simone asked. "You spent a lot of time in California, and Joe was in DC. How did you get together?"

"Well…" I stumbled a little and gave a chuckle. "Alaska is a very big state, geographically. But in many ways it's also very small. You get to know the people here." I took a breath, wondering where to go with this line of talking.

I almost gave in and did the nose touch and tuck my hair behind my ear signal. But then I met the warmth of Joe's gaze, and my mind flew back to our dinner and dessert and that first night we spent together.

I relaxed and couldn't help a small smile.

He smiled back.

"We hadn't seen each other for a while." I stuck to the truth. "And when we did, something clicked." I took another breath. "It just clicked, and we knew it was more than a friendship. What we were feeling went way beyond our family's relationship."

Joe's gaze warmed further and his eyes softened on me, and it felt like the rest of the world disappeared.

Simone cleared her throat. "Well… I guess we can all

appreciate a story like that. Thanks to you both for coming in today."

Joe finally broke our gaze, looking to Simone. "We were delighted to be here. Thank you for having us."

As the sound tech unclipped our microphones, and we slid from our high stools, Joe took my hand.

Charmaine, who had watched from the wings of the studio, was like a puppy full of energy and eagerness, telling us that social media was blowing up again. She swore they couldn't get enough of us, that we were an Alaskan royal couple—fresh young faces taking the lower forty-eight by storm.

I took her enthusiasm with a grain of salt. I knew she was paid to ramp up the excitement around Joe. But then Joe's phone rang, and he checked the screen.

"It's Bellamy," he said as we headed down a back hallway of the studio building toward the exit.

Charmaine's eyes got very round, and even I knew Joe had to be referring to House Leader Jerome Bellamy.

"Nice to hear from you, sir," Joe said as we all paused.

I looked up and down the hallway, wondering if this was a crisis and wondering if it was supposed to be confidential. There was no one in the hallway but us.

I pointed and whispered to Charmaine. "Should we get out of his way?"

She looked surprised by the question and shook her head. Clearly, she was intent on listening in.

"I appreciate that," Joe said into the phone. "Yes, we did." He didn't look shocked or concerned, so I concluded it wasn't a disaster or an emergency. "Absolutely," he said.

Charmaine and I looked at each other. It was clear neither of us had the slightest idea of what the conversation was about.

"Thank you," Joe said. "See you then."

Charmaine broke a grin and nudged me on the arm. By the sparkle in her eyes, I gathered *see you then* was a sign of something good.

"You're meeting with him?" she asked as Joe pocketed his phone.

"Dinner," Joe said, and Charmaine squealed.

"He's not going to do that unless—"

"Let's not get ahead of ourselves," Joe said.

"Unless what?" I asked, curious.

Charmaine grasped my shoulder. "Joe's in the running for committee chair. He's *really* in the running now."

Joe slid a guilty look my way. "I told him we'd come."

A cool wave of concern washed over me. "We?"

"I'm calling Hilda," Charmaine said, thumbing her screen. "When?" she asked Joe.

"Tonight," Joe said to me.

"We?" I repeated, knowing what he had to mean but affronted that he'd try to commit me like that. I'd flown all the way down here for the party, then I'd agreed to the interview and he was *still* pressing his luck.

"You don't say no to the leader," Joe said.

Charmaine shook her head in agreement. "You never say no to the leader."

"I do," I said. "He's not my leader."

Charmaine's expression fell. "Hang on," she said into her phone, then looked helplessly at Joe.

I could see I was causing a minor catastrophe.

"He wants to meet you," Joe said. "He saw the segment and liked it."

"I don't even remember everything I said." That wasn't my argument for going home today, but it was true.

"I don't want to push you," Joe said.

"But you just accepted an invitation on my behalf."

"I know you're not political," Joe said. "And this is my

thing, not yours. And you didn't sign up for all of this. But I'm a junior congressman—I don't tell the leader I'll have to call him back with an answer to his invitation."

"I have to go home," I said. "I have work to do. My work. To me, it's just as important as your work."

"I'll charter you a jet," Joe said.

Charmaine looked even more shocked by that.

"At personal expense," Joe said to Charmaine.

"No, I'm still here," Charmaine said into the phone.

"As soon as dinner's over, I'll drive you to the airport. On a private jet, you'll have a proper bed to sleep in for the trip back, and you can go to work in the morning like you planned."

When he put it that way, I felt churlish saying no. It was obviously important to Joe, to both of them. I wasn't heartless.

"Fine," I said.

"The congressman and his wife are having dinner with the House leader," Charmaine said breathlessly into the phone.

"But we have to talk first," I said to Joe in a no-nonsense tone.

"Sure." He answered seriously, but his eyes held a happy glow.

"I can't just sit there touching my nose and tucking my hair behind my ear through the whole dinner. Jerome Bellamy will think I'm unfriendly or rude."

"We've got hours."

"You've got that thing," Charmaine interrupted. "Lunch with the youth reps. And we better hurry and catch the flight back."

"After that," Joe said and started to walk for the exit again. "Just you and me. We'll sit down somewhere and—"

"The botanists are at three thirty. There's a photo op

in the park garden," Charmaine said. She was scrolling through her phone now, having disconnected from Joe's executive assistant, Hilda Newsome.

"Well, do I have five minutes somewhere to spend with *my wife*?"

"Sure, yes, of course." Charmaine scrolled. "I'll push the staff meeting so you'll have time to get ready for dinner."

"Just do what you have to do," I said to Joe, accepting that he was a ludicrously busy man. We'd exited to the sidewalk, and Joe's car pulled up to the curb.

"Push the staff meeting," he said to Charmaine.

The driver hopped out to open the back door, but Joe beat him to it, so the driver opened the front door for Charmaine.

"I need to find something to wear, anyway," I said. Plus, I'd need a few other necessities if I was going out for another evening.

"Cocktail dress? Separates? A black suit?" Charmaine spoke to me even while she kept reading things on her phone.

"I am capable of shopping," I told her, getting set to climb into the car.

She looked up. "Oh, sorry, habit."

Eight

My suitcase arrived in Windward five days after I got home. The airline called to say it would be delivered to my house in the evening. I could have lived with losing the nightgown, underwear and makeup, but I was happy to get back my go-to black dress and a favorite set of earrings.

I was reviewing preliminary theater sketches from six interior design firms. We wanted to get the decorating contract in place before the end of September. My front doorbell rang, and I went to answer, wondering if I should tip the driver or if the airline took care of that.

I retrieved a ten-dollar bill from my purse on the way, deciding better to be safe. So, the guy got a double tip. He was working an evening shift and could probably use a little extra. Then, on second thought, I switched to a twenty.

The driver knocked again just as I opened the door.

Sophie was standing on the porch. "Surprise!"

"What?" I looked behind her, still thinking I'd see the driver before realizing that was silly. Then I looked for Stone.

"I came for a visit." She was carrying a small suitcase.

My gaze went to her belly, which was slightly rounded under her sweater. "You look pregnant."

She laughed. "Are you going to let me in?"

"Yes. Yes, of course." I stepped back. "Where's Stone?"

"Back in Anchorage."

"You came by yourself?"

She set her bag down in the foyer. "Of course."

"Right. Of course. I don't know why I asked that." I shut the door behind her, embarrassed that I was buying into the fragile-pregnant-woman myth. I was pregnant, and I wasn't the least bit fragile.

"I came for some girl talk," she said.

"Is something wrong?"

"No." She studied my face for a second. "Is something wrong with you?"

"No. Did you hear something was wrong with me?" I gestured her toward the living room. "Leave the bag. We can take it upstairs later."

"I heard you went to DC," Sophie said, choosing to sit down in an armchair before kicking off her flats.

"That was quite the trip," I said, folding myself onto the end of the sofa. I was wearing a loose pair of low-waisted, softly worn jeans, an oversize T-shirt and a pair of thick knit socks to keep my feet warm.

"Stone talked to Joe yesterday."

I tried to imagine what Joe might have told Stone that would bring Sophie to Windward for a sudden visit. He and I had parted on perfectly amiable terms, even if it had been in a rush after the dinner with the House leader.

"Please tell me that's not why you're here," I said.

"I've been meaning to come for a while." She stretched her neck to look around. "I like this place, by the way. Funky."

"I keep finding little nooks and crannies everywhere. They've obviously tried to keep the antique authenticity of the house. But I think most people only stay for the weekend or a couple of weeks. It's not a place you could move into with all your stuff."

"Where's your stuff?"

"Back in Sacramento. Katie put it in storage for me."

"Are you going back there?"

I shrugged. "Probably not."

"You want to move it to the house in Anchorage? There's loads of room there."

That was always an option. The family house had a dozen bedrooms, a huge garage, a full basement and numerous outbuildings.

"Maybe," I said. "It's not a priority. I've been too busy to think about it."

"I guess, with the job, the baby and Joe all on your plate."

"Speaking of babies, you look *terrific*, Sophie." I pulled my T-shirt tight against my stomach. "I'm only just getting a little bit of a bulge."

Sophie grinned. "Oh, the growing will go fast now. Next you'll be getting kicked."

"Are you feeling movement?" I sometimes lay perfectly still at night and tried to feel something. So far, I hadn't felt a thing.

She nodded. "It's still faint. Stone said he could feel the kicking once, but I think he was imagining it."

For a moment, I felt jealous of Sophie's relationship with Stone. It would be nice to have the baby's father by your side experiencing all the stages. But I shook off the melancholy. My situation was what it was. Joe wasn't here with me, and here wasn't where he was supposed to be.

"Joe told Stone you were a big hit in DC."

I gave a chuckle remembering the surreal experience. "Charmaine, Joe's media assistant, was beyond thrilled with the coverage. Did he tell you we did an interview?"

"I saw it on the network's website."

"They posted it?" I don't know why I'd expected it to be a one-shot deal. It was slightly unnerving to know people could continue to watch me. I struggled again to remember what I'd said.

"You were great. Very poised, very articulate, very pretty."

"I can barely remember anything I said."

"Do you want to watch it again?"

"No!" I couldn't imagine anything more unnerving than watching my hesitations and missteps on a screen. "I'll just take your word for it that I pulled it off."

"Are you going back?" There was something off in Sophie's question. It sounded too casual, too smooth.

My suspicions were triggered. "Why?"

She shrugged. "It sounds like it was good for Joe to have you there."

"Did Joe send you?"

She looked insulted. "Would I come here as a spy? As Joe's spy?"

"No, but you might come here as Stone and Braxton's spy."

Sophie's husband was intensely loyal to my uncle Braxton, since Braxton had adopted him from the foster care system as a teenager and raised him as if he was his own. There wasn't much Stone wouldn't do for Braxton and Kodiak Communications, I knew that. And if Joe's success fostered Kodiak's success, and if Braxton had asked a favor of Stone, Stone might have enlisted Sophie in the effort.

"Never," she said emphatically. "I want what's best for you."

"I appreciate that." My mind was back on the DC trip now. "I guess Stone told you about the dinner with Jerome Bellamy."

"He mentioned it."

"According to Charmaine, it was epic."

Charmaine had followed up by phone earlier today, pushing me for more engagements. She was a tenacious, single-minded woman, and she didn't know Joe and I were anything but a simple married couple. It was frustrating to have to dance around the reasons for my reluctance to go back and see Joe.

"She says it's all part of the vetting process. For putting Joe's name forward as committee chair. She said it's a thing, him being so young and from Alaska. I know the committee work is important to him—they cover the kinds of things that got him into politics in the first place."

"So, that's good," Sophie said, clearly puzzled by my tone.

"They want me back. That's what's not good. The chair will be appointed at the end of next week, and they're saying I could help with a final push."

"Joe asked you to come back to DC?"

"Charmaine did. More like she hinted very strongly." I guessed by the way she danced around it that she was under Joe's orders not to outright ask.

"But that's not happening," Sophie said.

It wasn't a question, but I answered anyway. "No. I took a really big risk coming back to Alaska, because this job is so good for my career. I'm not compromising it by zooming off to DC every time Joe needs his plus-one."

Sophie's tone was dismissive, almost amused. "He does *not* call you his plus-one."

That was true.

"Has your boss complained?" she asked.

"No. He's a big fan of Joe's, especially now that the senator's on board with the arts and culture center funding."

"Okay." There was something critical in the tone of that word.

"What okay?"

"Nothing."

"What are you getting at?"

"It sounds like you wouldn't compromise your job if you helped Joe out, that's all."

"That's not what I said."

"It kinda is."

"You *are* a spy."

"No, no, no." She was shaking her head.

"Then why do you want me to become Joe's political helpmate?"

"Did I say that?"

"You're about to."

Sophie hesitated just long enough for me to know I was right. She was framing her answer. I'd seen her do that with Braxton. It was a tell that meant her answer was nuanced and meant to be persuasive.

"See?" I said, having proven my point.

"This thing with you and Joe—"

I couldn't help being flippant. "You mean the marriage thing?"

She cracked a smile at that. "It was supposed to benefit you both. It boosts Joe's political career and funds your construction project."

"Plus, the baby," I said, although she was mainly right.

"Yes, of course." Her tone softened. "The baby. The baby will be born in about six months. Your arts and culture complex will be well on its way to success by then. Don't you want Joe to get a boost, too? You know, before your deal comes to an end and you go your separate ways."

"I gave him a boost last week." I'd stepped up, and Joe had already been noticed by people in high places. They were considering him. I couldn't make him a better fit just by showing up.

"It sounds like the committee chair seat would be a real launching pad for him."

"Is that what he told Stone?" I asked.

"He did."

"See, I *knew*—"

"Stone didn't ask me to talk to you. Come on, Adeline, he'd never do that. But here's the thing. I'm thinking of you."

"Of me." My skepticism was clear.

"Yes. Once Joe is on a solid trajectory toward the governorship, you'll have more options. The higher his positive profile, the less impact your parting will have on his career."

I wanted to argue back. But what she said made a certain kind of sense. I knew this was how she'd always brought Braxton around to her way to thinking—by making sense.

"I know you, Adeline. You might rail against your family and their calculated plans, but you can't bring yourself to harm them. The more they need you, the more tempted you are to help." Her tone was heartfelt. "It's the same with Joe. The more he needs you…"

I opened my mouth, but then I shut it again. Sophie truly was on my side. It might be counterintuitive, but she was right. The better grip Joe had on the governor nomination, the less he needed me, and the freer I'd be to pursue my own dreams.

After Sophie left for Anchorage, I sat down with William to see if it was possible to take a few days off next week. Our team was expanding by the day, and between the architecture and engineering firms, construction companies, interior decorators, and the multitude of subcontractors, the day-to-day work was quite well in hand.

It helped that the community consultations were finished. So, when William and I put our minds to it, we realized I could work remotely for a few days without impacting progress on the project.

I waited until I got home that night to call Joe.

"Hello?" He sounded half-asleep, and I immediately felt guilty about the time zone difference.

"Did I wake you?" I asked.

"Adeline? Everything okay? The baby?"

"Everything's good. I'm fine. I'm sorry. I thought you'd still be up."

"I am up." He sounded more alert now. "I was reading a financial report on the sofa. I guess it got a little boring."

"Financial reports will do that to you." I could hear him moving around.

"How are things in Alaska?"

"Good, everything's good. We're even slightly ahead of schedule, which is useful, since we've only got a few weeks left until the snow falls." I didn't know why I was procrastinating. It wasn't like I had bad news.

"You'll want to be weathertight before November."

"Yes. Right. Joe—"

"Something *is* wrong."

"No. I'd tell you if it was. I've been talking with William and, well, I can manage a few days off next week if it helps. You know, for you. If it helps for me to fly down—"

"To *DC*?" He sounded stunned—not happy, just astonished.

"Yes. Maybe. That is, if you want me to." I wasn't getting the reaction I'd expected. Restless, I stood up and walked from my office into the living room.

"That's great!"

Okay. That was more along the lines I'd been thinking. "Yeah?"

"Come as soon as you can. Charmaine's going to jump for joy."

I swallowed and was suddenly thirsty, so I turned for the kitchen. "Oh, good. Not the Charmaine jumping for joy part. I don't think that's necessary. I mean the part where it's helpful."

His tone turned lower. "You know it's helpful."

"I thought it might be. I mean, last time we scored a good dinner invitation."

Joe was silent for a moment. "This means a lot to me, Adeline."

"I'm…" I chose my words. "Happy to help out. I want to help out."

"Next week would be perfect timing," he said.

"Tuesday work for you?" I poured myself a glass of ice water.

"Yes. I'll book a jet."

"You're not booking a jet."

"Oh, yes, I am."

"Joe."

"My pregnant wife is flying over three thousand miles to support my career. She's not taking the milk run through Anchorage and Dallas."

"It's more direct if you take the red-eye."

"You're not schlepping your way through three different airports again."

I had to admit, I did love the idea of skipping security, boarding in Windward then getting off at ExBlue airport. "Fine," I said, sounding more reluctant than I was feeling. "I mean, thanks. Thanks, Joe."

"Anytime. Literally, anytime."

I heard the background clink of an ice cube on his end. "What are you drinking?" I took my water back to the living room and picked out a comfy chair to sit down.

"Bourbon and water."

"I miss bourbon. Well, I miss wine more. But I'd take a bourbon right now. I've only got the water part."

He chuckled. "Want me to switch to plain water? Keep you company?"

"No." There seemed little point in that. "I want you to enjoy the bourbon for both of us."

We were quiet for a moment.

"How's the baby?" he asked.

"I felt a kick."

"You *did*?"

"Just a little one. More of a flutter, really." Emotion hitched in my chest then, and I felt the need to change the subject. "Sophie came to Windward for a couple of days."

"Stone said she was going to visit."

"He reported that to you?"

"It was random conversation. Stone's a great guy. I talk to him. He talks to Sophie."

"Well, aren't you three thick as thieves."

"You are definitely not writing my next campaign slogan." There was a thread of humor in his voice.

"Charmaine said they're naming the committee chair at the end of next week."

"You've been talking to Charmaine? Who's thick as thieves now?"

"She didn't ask me to come down." I paused, wondering if I wanted to press the subject. "You know, I feel like we've got go-betweens in our relationship."

"Does that surprise you?"

It didn't. But I didn't like it. We might not have a real

marriage, but we were both intelligent adults. We should be able to figure out how to communicate with each other.

"Adeline?" he prompted.

"Can we work on that?" I asked. "Eliminate the go-betweens? Just tell each other what we need."

This time it was Joe who paused. "Sure."

"You don't sound sure."

"We can work on that while you're down here."

"Between meetings and social events?" I asked, trying to lighten the mood but sounding sarcastic.

"What's really wrong?"

"Nothing. Just that. I guess I'm tired of trying to figure this thing out."

"You want to talk it through now?"

"No." It would be better in person. "Tell me what to expect when I get there. What are the events?"

"There'll be a formal thing Friday night after they announce— I mean, if you can stay that long."

"Sure." I decided if I was going to do this thing, I might as well go all the way.

I started to mentally compose my wardrobe and consider my schedule. My repatriated black dress, for sure, and something professional for any business functions. I had a pair of steel-gray slacks that were loose enough to still wear. I'd add my teal silk blouse and a classic black blazer. I felt a little thrill for a moment thinking about cute shoes. Practical footwear was standard in Alaska, and steel toes were required on the job site.

"There'll be various brunches, lunches or dinners," Joe said. "I think there's a presentation to a youth club Thursday afternoon. The kids are always great at those things. I don't know the whole itinerary, but does that help? Is that enough?"

"Yes."

We both went silent again.

Joe was first to break it. "I'm looking forward to seeing you."

"Me, too." Now that it was settled, I pictured myself in his DC condo…in his bedroom…in his white shirt…in his bed. My skin heated, and my breath hitched in my throat.

I was in DC by noon, and Joe picked me up at the airport. I was surprised by that. I'd expected him to make some arrangement, maybe a driver or even Charmaine. But I didn't expect him to break up what had to be a busy day and drive through traffic.

He hugged me, and I hugged him back, feeling the contours of his suit against my lightweight dress as the flight attendant loaded my bags into the trunk of his black sedan.

"No driver this time?" I asked as he opened the passenger door for me. It looked like the kind of car that should have a driver—sleek and black, polished to a high shine.

"I'm fully licensed in DC."

"I thought having a driver was a perk of the job." My dress fluttered against my legs.

"It's definitely a perk. Especially where parking's tight, or if I'm planning to have a drink or two, or if I'm getting dropped off at the airport and the car needs to go back without me."

I sat down on the comfortable leather passenger seat, and he rested his hand on the top corner of the door.

I couldn't resist teasing. "But if you sometimes have to drive yourself, you're clearly not as important as I thought."

"So sorry to disappoint you."

"Doing your own parking? Mingling with the common folk?" I asked on a doubtful expression.

"I'm more than happy to mingle."

"You're such a man of the people."

"The people are pretty great." He grinned as he shut the door and walked to the driver's side.

"So, they mostly love you?" I asked as I fastened my seat belt and he settled in.

He shook his head and drove forward. "I wouldn't go that far. But I'm not powerful enough to make them angry."

"Yet," I said.

"Yet," he agreed as we passed through the security gate.

"Something to look forward to, then."

He glanced sideways. "You don't have to worry, you know. People like you even better than they like me."

I fought an amused smile and gave him a mock salute. "Noted. Where are we going first?"

"The condo. I thought you'd want to drop off your bags, maybe freshen up."

"Sounds good. But you don't need to babysit me if you've got things to do this afternoon."

"I'm going to show you off," he said and smiled my way as we turned off the airport road and into traffic.

"In that case, I'm definitely freshening up."

Traffic grew heavier as we made our way down Massachusetts Avenue. The streets hummed with choreographed city life—the sounds, the traffic and the surge of pedestrians were all intriguing to me after the quiet of Windward.

We pulled up in front of Joe's brick building. He retrieved my suitcase and let us in the front door. Neither of us said anything about sleeping arrangements, and when he started up the stairs, I allowed myself to think about a night in his arms.

I followed, and he turned into his room.

"There's plenty of room in the closet," he said, setting down the bag. "And there are some empty drawers in the en suite. Do you need space in the dresser?"

"The closet's fine," I said, struggling to come to terms

with the intimacy of the situation. I decided to put first things first and dropped my purse on an armchair. "What should I wear today? And how much time do I have to change?"

He moved a little closer. "I thought we'd swing by the office first. Everybody wants to meet you. Charmaine keeps singing your praises."

"I hope I don't disappoint them." Experience told me Charmaine tended to be generous in her enthusiasm.

"How would you do that?" He shifted closer still, an amused little smile on his face. "Just do the usual thing. You know, be outgoing, erudite and witty. You are up-to-date on the trade negotiations with the EU relative to the aerospace industry, right?"

"Erudite?" I squared my shoulders and tipped up my chin. "I come from Alaska by way of California. We're laid-back and down-to-earth."

"Then you may have ended up in the wrong town."

"Ha-ha."

"Nobody's going to quiz you. Not that you wouldn't pass."

"I don't know a single thing about the EU aerospace industry."

"Neither does anyone else. Well, except for the negotiators. But they're way too serious to attend parties."

I wanted to kiss him. He had a unique magnetism up close like this, and I very desperately wanted to kiss him.

"What are you thinking?" His voice was husky, and it seemed like he could read my mind.

"Nothing," I lied.

"We were going to be up front with each other, remember?"

"Yes," I admitted. It had been my idea.

He took my hand gently in his. "So, then tell me what you're thinking."

I didn't want to do that. "It's really not…"

He shook his head, his features softening, a cute smile growing on his face. "Uh-uh. Put up or shut up, Mrs. Breckenridge."

"You go first," I countered. "What are you thinking?"

To my surprise, he didn't hesitate. "That I'm very glad to see you."

"Because I'll help with the committee chair appointment?"

"No." He playfully brushed his fingertip across the tip of my nose. "Because you're fun and adorable. Your turn."

My chest tightened and my breath hitched. I went with a partial truth. "That you're a very handsome congressman."

"That's a good start," he said, his tone lower still.

I felt myself sway toward him.

"Were you going to get changed?" he asked.

"I was."

"You should."

"I know."

We both stayed still, gazes locked.

He cupped my cheek in his palm, a glow coming up behind his eyes.

I tried not to lean into his touch, but the temptation was too much. I tipped my head to one side, drinking in the warmth of his broad palm.

He stepped forward and closed the gap. "Sex has always been the easy part for us."

He was right about that, and I was both relieved and gratified that he'd just thrown it out there. We were communicating. It was a start.

"We don't have time." My voice came out husky and breathless.

He wrapped an arm around my waist and eased me up against him. "Have a little faith."

I knew he was joking, but he kissed my neck while he slid my dress upward.

"Joe, we should—" I only got out the few words before desire flared to life inside me.

His kissed my lips then, and I instinctively kissed him back.

"I'm only helping," he said.

"Helping?" I tried not to laugh.

"You have to take it off to change." He eased the dress a little farther up my thighs.

"Are you telling me chivalry is not dead?"

"No, ma'am." His gaze was burning now, filled with hunger and passion.

My skin pebbled, arousal spearing deep within my core. I lifted my arms, and he peeled the dress upward, lifting it over my head and tossing it onto an armchair. I was wearing lilac lace with pink accents, little bikinis and a plunging bra.

He stepped back to look, then he feathered his fingertips over the small rounding of my stomach.

I looked down at the contrast between my smooth, pale stomach and his tanned, rough hand.

"You are *so* sexy," he rasped.

I was losing the battle to keep a hold of what little logic I had left. "Are we going to be late?"

"Yes." He came forward and swept me into his arms.

Our kisses were indulgent, then playful, then bordered on frantic as they deepened, and his hands splayed over my back. I was ready to fall onto the waiting bed. Ready to tear off his suit and fall naked into each other's arms all over again.

But Joe suddenly froze. He was breathing fast and his

eyes were dazed with passion. "We're going to be *very* late if we keep this up."

My mind stuttered for a second.

He'd actually meant for me to change my clothes? It wasn't a ruse to get me naked?

I shook myself back to reality. "Yes. Sure. I'll…" I waved in the general direction of my suitcase. "You know."

"Hey." He put his hand on my shoulder to stop me.

I willed my heart rate to slow and my hormones to settle.

"Later?" he asked.

I gave a nod.

He nodded back and took another look at my lacy underwear. "I'll be thinking about what's hiding under your dress all afternoon."

Since we were going straight from the office to a cocktail party on the top floor of the Vista Green Club, I'd put on a black three-quarter-sleeve blazer over a sleeveless royal blue dress with a lace neckline. The blazer covered my bare shoulders and the more elegant details of the dress, leaving the smooth skirt and scalloped above-the-knee hem showing beneath. I converted the look for evening by leaving the blazer in Joe's car.

Joe had introduced me to dozens of people; I was struggling hard to keep the names straight. I left him to continue schmoozing while I visited the ladies' room and picked up a glass of ginger ale. Watching him now, he cut an impressive figure in his tailored suit, taller than most of the other men, his broad shoulders and strong chin distinguishing him.

"We meet again," came a smooth masculine voice.

I turned my head to see Nigel beside me, an ironic smirk on his face and a highball in his hand—something with a swizzle stick, a cherry and an orange slice.

"Hello, Nigel." I wasn't friendly, but I wasn't rude, either.

"You're here with Joe?" His gaze followed mine across the ballroom.

"Of course." There was obviously no other reason for me to be in DC, never mind at this particular gathering.

"Governor Harland is meeting with the vice president."

"Uh, that's nice." I guessed from his tone that I was supposed to be impressed.

Joe was approached by another group of people, all smiling and shaking his hand.

"I thought I'd check out what was going on here," Nigel said, taking a sip of his drink.

I sipped my ginger ale. It was cool against my dry throat.

"You know we're on to you, right?" Nigel asked, his tone going darker, the fingers of his free hand drumming the rim of his glass.

"On to what?" I asked, a hum of anxiety creeping over my skin.

"Don't play coy. This little charade you've got going with Breckenridge. The voters don't like being conned, Adeline."

"You don't think we're married?" I decided to go on offense in the hopes of covering the kernel of truth in his accusations.

He scoffed and gave me an eye roll.

"We had five hundred witnesses," I pointed out.

"How long do you think you can keep this up?" His gaze went to my stomach.

Surely he didn't think I was faking a pregnancy. "What is it you want, Nigel?" There were dozens if not hundreds of interesting people at this party. I didn't need to stand here listening to Nigel's accusations.

"Me? Nothing. But you should know the governor has

connections, spies, if you will, and it's a long time until the next governor's election."

"Enjoy the party, Nigel," I said and took a step away.

He shot forward, his face only inches from mine. "Be warned—"

"Back away from my wife," Joe growled, coming into my view.

Nigel looked up, and his expression fell.

Joe had a good four inches on Nigel and wore the most serious expression I'd ever seen.

Nigel retreated instantly. "I was just saying hello."

Joe stepped to my side. "You okay?"

"I'm fine." I nodded. I was more annoyed than anything else.

Nigel shifted awkwardly. "I'll just be—"

"Leaving the party?" Joe asked, his intonation making it clear that it wasn't really a question.

"Yes," Nigel said. "I'm meeting up with the governor. Good night."

We watched him walk away, quickly disappearing into the crowd.

"The governor is in town to meet with the vice president," I told Joe.

"You sure you're okay?"

"He didn't even touch me." I was okay. Really.

"What did he say?"

"That he was on to us. He wants to know how long we think we can keep up the facade."

Joe looked puzzled. "What facade?"

"You know what facade." Sure, we were really married, but Nigel had obviously heard or guessed that it wasn't a romantic, honest, until-death-do-us-part marriage.

The conversation ebbed and flowed around us, drink

glasses clinking, people laughing, plenty of hearty smiles and crisp handshakes.

"There's no way he knows anything," Joe said.

"He told me they had spies."

"He's bluffing."

I wasn't so sure.

"Who would spy?" Joe asked. "Sophie? Stone? Your brothers? Katie?"

"None of them," I said. And it sure wouldn't be my dad or Braxton.

"There are a limited number of people who know the finer points of our situation."

"Still…" I couldn't help worrying a little bit.

"He name-checked the vice president?" There was a thread of amusement in Joe's tone now.

"I got the distinct impression this was the B-list event."

"Then he's a B-lister, too, since he wasn't the one rubbing shoulders with the VP."

"I should have called him on that."

Joe's arm went around me for a moment. "Let's forget about him."

I remembered something else. "He said the voters don't like being conned. It sounded like a threat, like he was going to reveal something."

"He was fishing. Our relationship happened fast. That's all he has to go on. Let's find Charmaine."

I was confused by the change of subject. "Does she need something?"

"A strong offense is the best defense." He took my hand.

I did a hop-step as he started walking.

It took us thirty minutes and four conversations to make our way across the ballroom to Charmaine. She spotted us coming and met us.

"Congressman," she greeted Joe. She was dressed impeccably, a shimmering, off-the-shoulder green cocktail sheath that flowed to just below her knees.

"You want to do a little social media?" he asked.

Her eyes lit up. "Absolutely. What do you have in mind?"

"How about some video footage?"

"I'll get us a camera operator."

"No, no. I want it to look casual, clandestine. Can you post it from somewhere nonofficial?"

"I'm liking your style, boss."

I viewed Joe with curiosity, surprised he'd gone all covert operative.

"We need a quiet corner," he said, looking around.

"Over there," Charmaine said. "Between the plant display and the dais."

"That'll work," Joe said, looping his arm around my waist.

"What are we doing?" I asked as we started walking.

The room was full, and a few people tried to get his attention as we made our way through the crowd, but Joe gave them a smile and a wave and kept on walking.

"Shouldn't you be chatting them up?" I asked.

"They'll still be there when we're done."

"Done what?" I was still in the dark about his plan.

Charmaine didn't have much information, either, but she didn't seem remotely concerned. She'd tucked herself in behind Joe, letting us clear her a path while she did something on her phone.

"This'll do," he said and came to a halt.

"What—"

He put his hands on my shoulders and turned me slightly sideways, then he mussed my hair a little in the front.

I couldn't help but smile. "Why are you messing me up?"

"I'm making you look casual. Pinch your cheeks."

"Are you serious?"

"Flushed is good," Charmaine said, looking me over. She reached forward and straightened my necklace, then pulled the right shoulder of my dress slightly askew.

I pinched my cheeks. "Exactly *what* are we doing here?"

She grinned happily. "How far away do you want me?"

"I don't want any sound," Joe said. "Just make the framing nice."

"Got it." She looked over her shoulder and took several steps back.

"Look happy," he whispered.

I couldn't do anything but look happy, since this felt so silly.

"Gaze into my eyes," he said.

I did.

"Now think about the baby."

I could feel my expression soften.

He leaned in and put his mouth close to my ear. "I'm going to touch your stomach," he whispered. "Give me a really slow smile." He pressed his warm palm against my stomach, cradling the small bulge. "I can't wait to feel the first kick," he said.

I tried to give him the slow smile, but emotion was so thick and tight in my chest that I had to blink.

"You're the best," he whispered and drew me into an enveloping hug in slow motion.

I wrapped my arms around his neck, all but soaked in the emotion.

"That," Charmaine said, walking back to us, "was *sensational*. Adeline, you deserve an Academy Award." She held up the phone and played the clip for us. "I swear, she had a tear in her eye."

Joe grinned. "Take that, Governor Harland."

I quickly shook my equilibrium back into place.

"The governor's here?" Charmaine asked, looking around.

"No, but his staff's been trash-talking our marriage."

Her fingers worked fast on her screen. "You two are a little bit scary."

"It's not me," I protested.

"That's why I love working for you," she said to Joe. She touched the screen with a flourish. "This is going to be fun to watch."

Nine

Joe was appointed to the committee chair position, and Nigel went quiet. In Windward, construction crews all made their deadlines, so the arts and culture center was ready for the harsher weather when the snow started to fly. As it piled up, I made a few more trips to DC, attending events with Joe so Charmaine could keep up our social media posts and make us look like happy newlyweds. Funny thing was, I *was* a happy newlywed.

I looked forward more than I should have to sleeping in Joe's arms. But I pushed away the niggling worry. Joe was a good conversationalist and a great dancer, and he knew a lot of interesting people. And it seemed to me that Sophie's plan was working, since Joe seemed to be in constant demand by the movers and shakers of his political world.

Things were running smoothly enough on the construction project that we dropped to a skeleton crew over the holidays, and I decided to spend them in Anchorage with

Joe and my family. Charmaine enlisted Sophie as her temporary photographer, and Sophie posted shots of happy pregnant me and solicitous husband Joe in front of the twenty-foot family Christmas tree, then outside walking in the snow.

We got a sunny, relatively warm day and hitched a sled up to a team of horses. Then we took some very romantic shots outside in the snow. Sophie and I went for a sleigh ride while Joe and Stone went riding with my brothers. He was sexy dressed up as a cowboy, and, after the ride, we cuddled around a bonfire sipping hot chocolate under the bright stars.

Katie came up to spend New Year's. On our last day, Sophie, Katie and I settled in the cozy den in front of the gas fireplace for some girl chat, even if Katie did roll her eyes at some of the pregnancy talk. Snow was falling outside the windows, and there was a panoramic view of the fat flakes outside the windows. I was going back to Windward soon, Joe going back to DC. I was sorry to see the holidays end.

When Stone got home and our chat broke up, I went in search of Joe, wanting to catch the final hours of our last day together in what felt like a happy paradise.

I heard Braxton's voice and guessed Joe was with him. They were beyond the stone fireplace in the great room, just out of my view.

"Right behind our backs," Braxton said with disgust.

"Harland could be lying," my dad put in.

"He knows too much for it to be a bluff," Joe said.

"And he got it from somewhere," Braxton agreed.

"They'll throw everything they've got at us. They won't pull their punches." Joe's voice got louder as I drew closer.

"But a spy?" my dad asked, incredulously.

"Can you come up with another explanation?" Braxton asked—demanded, really.

"Here?" Joe asked. "In your house?" He looked up and saw me. "Adeline," he said, toning himself down. It was framed as a greeting, but I knew he was alerting my father and my uncle to my presence.

Their backs to me, both older men turned.

"What's going on?" I asked them all.

"Just a little chitchat," Braxton said.

"You're going with *that*?" I counted incredulously. Then I looked at Joe, challenging him to lie to me, too.

"What did you hear?" Joe asked.

"Oh, no, no, no." I waved his question off. "That's not how this is going to work. What's Governor Harland doing?"

The three men all looked at each other.

I crossed my arms, tempted to tap my foot. "You can't come up with a plan while I'm standing right here," I told them.

Joe rose and came to me. "I don't want you to worry."

"I'm not some delicate little flower."

"You're six months pregnant."

"And it hasn't affected my brain."

"We think there's a spy in the house," Braxton whispered.

Joe and my dad glared at him.

"She wants the truth," Braxton said.

"In the house? This house?" I couldn't help lowering my voice, too, and glancing over my shoulder.

"The governor's office knows way too much about the family's personal business," Joe explained. "Someone's been feeding them information."

"I thought Nigel was bluffing," I said.

"Nigel?" Braxton asked.

"Back in September," Joe said. "Nigel Long was bragging that they were onto us."

"It sounds like they were."

"Who here would cooperate with Nigel?" I asked.

It wasn't a family member, that was for sure. And I couldn't imagine it was Sebastian or Marie or someone who'd been with us for years. Maybe someone temporary had overheard a conversation or two.

"*That's* what we're about to figure out," my dad said.

"How?" I asked, thinking Joe and I should have taken it more seriously back then, feeling partially responsible.

"It's not an insurmountable problem," Joe said, looking into my eyes.

"I want to help," I told him.

"You can help just by acting as you normally would."

"You mean fake normal, pretend-marriage normal."

"Assume people could be listening."

"This is creeping me out," I admitted. I hated the thought that I couldn't let my guard down even inside the house.

"That's what I wanted to avoid," Joe said.

"Coddling me was a bad plan. We should tell everybody." My brothers, Sophie, Katie—any one of them could give something away in front of a staff member or acquaintance.

"We will," Braxton said. "Carefully."

I nodded, agreeing with that. Then I glanced around again, wondering if there were microphones hidden in the lamps.

"We'll sweep for electronics," my dad stated.

It seemed overly dramatic, but I realized it was way too easy these days to hide a listening device anywhere.

Another thought occurred to me. "Maybe they hacked

our phones, turned them into hot mics. I read where you can do that."

"It's harder than you think," Joe said. "But we'll check that, too."

"What is wrong with people?" I asked rhetorically.

"All you have to do is go back to what you were doing," Joe said. "What were you doing just now?"

"Thinking I could use a snack."

"You want me to get you something?"

"No. I can do it. That would be what I'd normally be doing."

"Then carry on." Joe touched my arm and leaned in, giving me a kiss on the hairline.

I took a breath and gave myself a bracing mental shake, settling the new information into my brain as I headed for the kitchen.

I couldn't help padding quietly over the carpet, glancing around, wondering if someone was peeping around a corner at me, watching what I was doing.

"I do not want to keep sneaking around," Katie said as I approached the entryway.

The words stopped me cold. No way did she mean what it sounded like she meant.

"Nobody cares." It was Mason's voice, and when I eased forward, I saw he was leaning, hip braced against the breakfast island.

Everybody cared. I couldn't see Katie, but my brain reeled with the notion that my brother and dear friend could be plotting against us. It simply wasn't possible.

"I care," Katie said, sounding impatient.

"Then what do you want to do?" he asked, straightening and moving.

I eased farther forward to see him go to her, standing at the coffee maker.

"I don't know," she said, sounding distraught.

Stunned to my toes, I was about to march in and demand answers when Mason reached to smooth her hair.

His voice went lower, smoother, deeper. "Ignore it?"

"Maybe."

"No." There was a chuckle in his voice. "Not an option." He kissed her.

He kissed her, and she kissed him back, and reality hit me with a wave of relief.

They weren't spying on Joe and me. They were falling for each other.

I started to step back, but Mason saw the movement.

He jolted from Katie and stared straight at me. Regret flashed in his eyes. "Sorry."

I was relieved and surprised and happy for them all at the same time. "For liking Katie?"

Hearing my voice, she whirled around, looking guilty.

I continued talking to my brother. "I like Katie. I like her a lot."

Her face was flushed as she stared at me. "We——"

"You don't have to explain," I said. "I get it. And I respect your privacy and my brother's."

"We don't know what it is," she said.

"It's very...new," Mason finished.

"You both seemed into each other the first night you met," I pointed out, thinking I should have guessed back then. They'd started off sparring but then were the last ones to leave the balcony.

They glanced self-consciously at each other, and I realized I was intruding on a highly intimate conversation. I raised my palms and took a step back. "Forget I was here."

But Katie stepped forward. "Adeline——"

"Don't worry. It's not like Joe and I don't have a complicated romance."

Mason's attention shifted to something behind me.

Joe's hands closed gently over my shoulders. He leaned down, humor threading his tone. "*This* is you doing fake normal?"

It was anticlimactic to discover the culprit was a temporary cook's assistant gossiping to someone with a girlfriend in the governor's office. It wasn't a sophisticated spy network, and there were no hidden microphones in the house. There was also no malware in our phones, so we were able to go back to our usual behavior.

Katie liked Mason, and Mason liked Katie, but with so many miles between them, it was hard for their relationship to go further than that.

I was working long hours with the decorating team as they installed the millwork, finished the walls and finalized the flooring and furniture choices. Theater seats were on their way from Europe, while the lighting was backordered, and we were struggling to find an installation specialist for the sound system.

Sophie and Stone's baby was due in less than a week, so we were all on alert, and I was making sure I had my phone with me every minute.

William and I stood on the concrete floor of the main complex. Though we wore steel-toed boots, hard hats and vests, we stayed back from the scaffolding where workers were installing the drop ceiling.

"The planters will curve around the staircase," Maddy, the head interior designer, was telling us. "I want to bring them out three feet at the apex to give us room for larger trees. With the clear stories above, we could have a real conservatory space with benches, tables and a cobblestone walkway."

My phone pinged, and I immediately thought of Sophie

going into labor. My stomach contracted in what I assumed was a sympathy pain, and I smiled to myself as I discreetly pulled the phone from my pocket to check the screen.

It was a business text, not about Sophie.

I sighed my disappointment and tuned back into Maddy.

"I don't see a problem with the traffic flow," she said, walking partway across the room to show how much space would be left as a result of her suggestions. She raised her voice. "It wouldn't interfere with event lineups to the main desk. And it would give such a nice interior space for winter. Imagine, real greenery and a parklike atmosphere in January."

Since it was February now and bitterly cold, I had to agree with her on that.

I felt another twinge in my stomach and shifted my stance. I wondered if cousins could be psychically connected during childbirth. Maybe I'd hear from Sophie any minute now. Maybe she and Stone were already on their way to the hospital in Anchorage.

"As a reflection of the main space," Maddy said. "Let me show you what I was thinking for the retail area." She started to walk that way.

I looked at William to gauge his thoughts, wondering if he'd be open to a change at this stage of construction. There was time to do it, although we did need to watch our budget. A change here, an upgrade there, and we were moving into our contingency funds.

I fell into step with him several feet behind Maddy. "What's your—" A sharper pain crossed my stomach, and I gasped, stopping to cover it with my hand.

That had *hurt*.

"Adeline?" William asked, concern in his tone.

"Something's weird," I said, still thinking of Sophie.

"Do you need to sit down? Some water?"

"Maybe." Sitting down sounded like a good idea.

He pointed to a card table and two folding chairs near the bottom of the staircase.

Maddy had stopped and was looking back at us.

When she saw where we were headed, she came our way. "Everything all right?"

"Fine," I answered even though a low-grade soreness had settled into my stomach.

I sat down, and she crouched in front of me.

"Is it the baby?" she asked.

"I don't think so. It's way too soon. My cousin Sophie is—" The sudden sharp pain gripped me again, and I groaned.

"Call an ambulance," Maddy blurted to William.

"That's overkill," I said, but thinking maybe I would call my doctor.

"It might be," Maddy agreed. "But let's not take any chances."

I slipped my phone out of my pocket again and pulled up my doctor's office contact. "Dr. Reed," I said to both of them.

"Good idea," Maddy said, but she made a phone sign to William at the same time, and I knew they were calling for an ambulance.

I was slightly embarrassed, especially now that we'd caught the attention of some of the construction workers.

"Reed Clinic," Jill the receptionist answered.

"Jill, it's Adeline."

"Oh, hey, Adeline." Jill's voice was cheerful. "How are you doing?"

"Okay," I answered. "Well, a little funny."

Her tone immediately changed. "Funny how?"

"A few pains in my stomach."

"Sharp or dull?"

"A little of both." A sharp one hit me again, and I clenched my teeth.

"Adeline?"

"I'm here." My tone was tight, and I could feel sweat breaking out on my skin.

"Can you come in this afternoon?"

Maddy held out her hand for my phone.

It seemed easier just to hand it over.

"This is Maddy Schmidt. I'm with Adeline now, and we've called for an ambulance." Maddy stopped to listen. "I agree." She paused again. "Sounds good. We'll meet her there." She ended the call and handed back my phone.

"No more messing around," she told me sternly.

I could already hear the ambulance siren. The sound was gathering even more attention from the workers.

"I can walk," I said and started to get up.

Maddy put her hand on my shoulder. "Sit."

"That's an order," William added as he strode for the front door to meet the paramedics.

"Well, this is embarrassing," I said to Maddy.

"You're doing what's best for the baby."

I decided to think of it that way and nodded, even as a man and a woman dressed in navy blue uniforms wheeled a stretcher my way.

They helped me on board and immediately took my blood pressure.

The woman cupped my stomach with her hands. "Contractions?"

"I don't think so."

She kept still for a couple of minutes, then another pain hit, and I tensed up.

"I felt a tightening," she told me gently.

"That was me," I said.

"How old are you?" she asked.

"Twenty-eight."

"How many weeks pregnant?"

"Thirty-six."

She keyed her radio. "I have a twenty-eight-year-old female patient, thirty-six weeks pregnant, showing signs of premature labor."

"I'm not." I shook my head and reached for her arm to stop her. I didn't want people getting ahead of themselves on this.

"Her doctor's en route to the hospital," Maddy told the paramedics.

"I don't think I'm in labor," I told the paramedic. Technically, I knew it was possible. But these pains weren't all that bad. I'd had worse with the flu.

"Try to relax," she told me. "We're going to take good care of you."

The stretcher started to move, and I closed my eyes to keep from getting dizzy.

They loaded me into the ambulance, and in minutes we were pulling up to the back entrance of the hospital.

To my surprise, Dr. Reed got into the ambulance. My first thought was they'd realized there was no point in taking me inside. It was a relief. I had a lot of work left on my desk. In fact, my purse was still in my office. I needed to go back for it.

I started to sit up, but Dr. Reed stopped me.

"You're just fine right where you are," she said.

"I need to get my purse."

"Someone can pick it up for you." She put her hands on my stomach.

"So, I don't need to go inside?" The pains had subsided.

She didn't answer, just smiled and checked a tablet that the paramedic handed her. "Have you felt anything like this before?" she asked me.

"They're gone now," I said.

"Was this the first time?"

I nodded, then the pain came back, and I gritted my teeth.

The doctor nodded to the paramedic. "Let's call an H-flight."

The name registered in my mind—the Alaska Air Ambulance service.

"What?" I asked in confusion.

"You're in labor," Dr. Reed said in a steady reassuring voice. "Protocol is the Anchorage hospital before thirty-six weeks."

"I am thirty-six weeks."

"You're not quite over the wire yet. The good news is, this is early labor, so you've got plenty of time."

"I'm having the baby?" I was struggling to wrap my head around that.

"I'll have Jill call Joe to let him know."

"Joe's in DC." I knew Joe was going to flip out over this. He'd planned to come to Alaska two weeks early to make sure he didn't miss the birth.

Things got blurry for me after the air ambulance landed in Anchorage. I remembered a ride to the hospital and moving from the stretcher to a bed. For some reason Sophie showed up. She held my hand and talked me through the intensifying pains, telling me Joe was coming and would arrive soon.

Then Stone showed up and took Sophie away, and I was annoyed, since she'd been helping me breathe. I went into what felt like self-hypnosis for a while. A new nurse came in and checked me out.

Then I was hit with the urge to push. The nurse was kind, so was the doctor. But I wanted Joe and I wanted Sophie, my dad, too. And I wanted the pain to stop already. But I pushed hard, and when they put the tiny baby girl in my arms, my heart nearly burst from my chest with joy.

Joe rushed into the delivery room, a mask on his face, a cap on his head and a green gown flapping around him.

He came to a screeching halt when he saw us.

"You made it," I said, feeling a tear squeak out of the corner of my eye.

"Almost," he said, his gaze going to Matilda.

In my head, I'd already named her. I didn't know why. We hadn't even talked about names.

"Close enough," I rasped around a dry throat. "I only just met her this minute."

He put a hand on her little head, and his voice shook. "She's beautiful. You're beautiful." He leaned down to kiss my forehead. Then he kissed Matilda's.

The nurse gently took her from my arms. "I promise I'll bring her right back."

I watched them go, feeling euphoric now that the labor pains had stopped. "She was early," I said.

"Are you doing okay? Need anything?"

"Water," I said.

He looked around and found a pitcher and a glass, giving me a sip through a straw.

"It was something." I winced, remembering the waves of pain that had blocked out the world. "Sophie was here. But then she left."

"She's in labor."

"Now?"

Joe nodded.

"Poor thing." I felt a wave of sympathy. I sure wouldn't want to go back to those labor pains.

The nurse returned with Matilda wrapped in a pink blanket with a little pink cap on her head. Her face was so sweet—blue eyes, a tiny nose, a little bow of a mouth that moved. She didn't cry, just blinked like she was absorbing everything around her.

"Dad?" the nurse asked in a singsong voice, holding her out.

"You sure?" Joe asked me, looking scared.

I nodded and gave him a smile, my heart filling again as he took the tiny bundle in his big hands.

"She weighs nothing," he said in awe.

"Six pounds, three ounces," the nurse told him.

While Joe stared at the baby and whispered silly words, the nurse helped me into a fresh gown and changed the bedding around me, tucking me in with heated blankets before she left. The warmth felt heavenly.

"Hello, baby girl," Joe was saying. "Hello."

"I think she's Matilda," I said.

He looked at me in surprise.

"Is that okay?" I asked. "I took one look at her, and that's what the name was."

"It's absolutely okay," he said. "Matilda, would you like to go see your mommy now?" He gently put her into my arms.

I held her warm little body against my heart, checking out her face, her hands, counting her fingers. I leaned my head back against the upright mattress, sighing in pure bliss.

With the warmth all around me, my eyelids grew heavy, and I felt Joe's hand slip beneath Matilda.

"Maybe I should take her," he said softly.

I managed a nod as I drifted off.

I heard my dad's voice in the distance, followed by Joe's and Mason's.

Then I must have slept for a while, because a baby's cry woke me and a nurse was telling me Matilda was hungry.

I successfully fed her and felt relief. They'd moved a bassinet into the room, and I tucked her in, sitting down in the armchair beside it to drink some juice and then a big glass of water. I was incredibly thirsty again.

The door opened, and I looked up, expecting Joe to be back. But it was Stone.

He had a huge grin on his face and a little blue bundle in his arms.

I laughed out loud. "You have a baby!"

Matilda stirred but didn't wake up.

"How's Sophie?" I asked.

"She's great. Two doors down. Sleeping right now."

"Let me see," I said, starting to rise.

"Stay put," Stone said, coming my way and crouching down. "This is Lucas Nathaniel."

I didn't know if it was my maternal hormones kicking in, but Lucas Nathaniel was just about the most handsome baby boy I'd ever seen. "We don't have a middle name yet."

"That's because sweet Matilda was in such a hurry to get here. Love that name, by the way."

"You talked to Joe." I guessed a lot had happened in the three hours I'd slept, including Lucas.

"He went for a coffee with Braxton and Xavier. They're over-the-moon giddy about being grandfathers on exactly the same day."

"My dad, giddy? And *Braxton*, giddy? I'm having a hard time picturing that."

"You'll see it for yourself soon enough."

I reached out and touched Lucas's hand. "Congratulations, Stone."

"Congratulations to you, too." He checked out Matilda. "She's beautiful. You did good, Adeline."

The door opened again, and this time it was Joe.

"The party's in here," he said softly.

"Have you seen Lucas?" I asked him.

"I have."

Stone straightened. "I better go back to Sophie."

"Can I visit her?" I asked. I felt perfectly strong enough to walk down the hall.

"I'll let you know when she wakes up," Stone said, then nuzzled Lucas's cheek before heading out the door.

Joe rested his hand on Matilda's back. "Do you want to lie back down?" he asked me.

"I'm happy sitting. I wouldn't mind some more water."

"You bet." He went to the bedside table for the jug sitting there. The ice cubes clinked together as he poured some into my glass.

We gazed at each other in silence for a long time.

"So, now what?" I asked. I felt like we'd skipped over a month of planning.

"Now—well, tomorrow morning, the nurse said—the three of us go back to the house. Xavier and Braxton have a surprise for you."

"A crib, I hope." So far, Matilda didn't even have a place to sleep.

"A crib, yes. And a nursery. Well, a new bedroom for you with a nursery attached. They were already renovating for Sophie and Stone, so they doubled up."

I was happy about the crib. I wasn't one hundred percent sure on switching my bedroom for a nursery suite. It seemed abrupt, somehow. It was silly, given the circumstances, but a shimmer of déjà vu ran through me at the thought of my dad and Braxton planning my maternity leave.

"Adeline?" Joe asked, worry in his tone.

"I'm good." I pushed away the negative reaction and gave him a smile. "I'm great."

Ten

Matilda and Lucas grew fast. Just over three months old, they were smiling, shaking rattles and starting to roll over. Both had doubled their birth weights, and they interacted more and more with their grandfathers, laughing and cooing. They were utterly fascinated with each other.

Joe had offered to sleep in my old bedroom, leaving the new two-room nursery suite to me and Matilda. But he'd ended up in my room every night for the first few weeks, holding and rocking a fussy Matilda. Soon he was crawling into bed with me, holding me close like we'd done in DC. And once we started making tender love in the quiet wee hours of the morning, it was hard to stop.

He had to work in DC but logged a whole lot of miles traveling back and forth as much as he could.

Matilda fussed at night, but she took long naps during the day, giving me time to check on emails or make calls to the project supervisors in Windward. I was technically on maternity leave, so I stuck to an advisory capacity, but I loved getting progress reports and new pictures as the facility came together.

The snow melted away, and the sun was warm these days, bringing green shoots up on the lawn and out in the horse paddock. The babies were napping, with Marie watching them, and Sophie had suggested a horseback ride. We liked getting outside in the sunshine, and she was loving learning to ride.

I put Sophie on Splendor, since she was such a sweetheart, and I took Galahad for myself. The two horses were best friends and loved being together.

Barney, the stable manager, kindly tacked the horses up for us, since our time was limited before the babies woke up hungry. But we headed out the gate down to the river trail. My thigh muscles protested a bit. I hadn't done this much riding in years.

"It's so nice to get out," Sophie said as we walked the horses side by side. She inhaled deeply.

"You're good for me," I said with a smile.

At first, I'd been reluctant to leave Matilda alone for more than five minutes, worrying she'd get upset and want her mommy, but Sophie had encouraged me to push it a little. And Marie assured me she knew how to soothe a fussy baby. Now I appreciated our little escapes.

"How am I doing?" she asked.

I checked her posture. "Straighten your back a little." She did.

"Not too stiff," I warned her.

"It's hard to be straight without being stiff."

I smiled, understanding her complaint. "Splendor will feel your tension. Elbows a little closer in."

She moved them.

"That looks good," I said. "You want to trot?"

"Sure," she said, bracing herself.

"You're stiff again," I warned.

"I'm about to bounce up and down."

"Would you rather just walk?" There was no rush. The horses were always here, and Sophie had plenty of other teachers between Stone and my brothers.

"I want to learn faster," she said.

"That's not the way it works. It's better not to rush."

"So, we can walk, and I'll still be learning."

"Absolutely. Look, the robins are back."

"That's a good sign?"

"A good sign of spring." The sun was warm on my back, and the sky was a beautiful blue. Tiny leaf buds were coming out on the trees. With the longer days, the forest would be bright green in a couple of weeks.

The winters might be long in Alaska, but you couldn't beat the summers.

We did the river loop, coming back up at the far end of the paddock, crossing the field to the stable.

"Blue flag up," Sophie said, and we broke into a trot.

We'd worked out a signal system with Marie. A blue flag on the balcony meant Lucas needed his mommy. A pink flag meant Matilda needed me.

We slowed and stopped the horses in front of the stable. Sophie dismounted and handed me Splendor's reins.

"See you up there," she said, heading through the soft dirt to the gate.

I moved to dismount and led both horses forward, hoping to meet Barney and hand them off. There might not be a pink flag flying, but I felt an urgency to get back to Matilda.

I came to the open stable door and heard voices.

"Whatever it takes to keep her happy," my dad said.

I was still thinking about Matilda, and I agreed with her grandpa.

"You know I'm already doing that." It was Joe who answered.

I agreed on that front too. He was a wonderful daddy.

"This next phase is the crux of it all," Braxton said.

The next *phase*? My brain stumbled over the phrase.

"We still have six months left, Joe said."

"The real clock started back in January."

"It's not like we've been slacking," Joe said dryly. "The perfect Alaska family is a huge lift for the effort."

"No complaints there," my dad said in a hearty, placating tone.

Unease gripped my chest.

Galahad shook himself, jangling the tack.

"We should sit down with your team soon and map it out," Braxton said.

I heard the creak of leather and realized at least one of them was mounting up.

"I like that Charmaine," Braxton added. "She's got her eye on the prize."

There was a warning in Joe's tone. "I'm not rushing Adeline out on the campaign trail."

"Who's talking about rushing?" my father said. "But talk to William about timing. Because the longer she stays in Anchorage, the better for us. We can run things from here, set up some early events."

"Family friendly," Braxton put in, and I could hear the satisfied smile in his voice.

My dad gave a chuckle. "Whoever my daughter doesn't charm, my granddaughter sure will. Although when you get seriously out on the trail, you might want to think about a nanny."

"Does she even have to go back to Windward?" Braxton asked. "It sounds like they're doing just fine there without her."

"It's not like the funding's going to disappear," my dad added.

"True," Joe said. "Nigel is laser-focused on the governor's race right now. He won't mess with the project funding."

Shocked, I took a step back, not wanting to hear any more plans the trio of traitors had for my life. Splendor nuzzled my shoulder, pushing my Stetson askew.

"Great," my dad said heartily.

"We're in agreement," Braxton said back.

Joe started to speak, but Barney arrived.

"All done?" he asked me.

"I'm done," I said, feeling shell-shocked, with a driving urge to get back to Matilda and run.

I made it back to the house and into the bedroom, pushing the door closed and leaning back against it. Matilda was still sleeping, so I showered, scrubbing hard, trying to forget what I'd heard and what it meant.

As I dressed and dried my hair, the old feelings of manipulation and betrayal came over me. The worst part was it was my own fault. I'd blithely and happily gone along with their plans.

I'd stuck around for three months, three long months. I'd all but made my marriage to Joe real. We were essentially living as husband and wife. We were sleeping together, raising Matilda together, making glorious love whenever we could.

We hadn't talked about the future, but my plans hadn't changed. I was finishing the Windward project. Then I was moving on to my next urban planning job. I didn't know where it would be, but I wanted to be able to pursue it, with Matilda, whatever it was.

Annoyed with myself, I went to my computer. I brought up my CV and started on an update. The Windward project wouldn't end for several months, but I felt better, more in control, planning for the long term.

I decided to pick a company name, set myself up properly as a business. Maybe I'd use my initials, AEC Planners, something straightforward like Urban Planners, or maybe something northern, a nod to Alaska, since that experience had already proved valuable. Plus, it would be unique. Then again, it was too niche.

Matilda woke up, and I changed her.

In my newfound zeal, I'd discovered I could calm a baby while typing. So, I updated my CV, registered AEC Urban Planners as a business, designed a basic logo, ordered a thousand business cards and composed an email to William telling him I'd be returning to Windward ASAP.

The bedroom door opened, and Joe sauntered in wearing blue jeans and a plaid button-down shirt. "There you are." He lowered his voice when he saw Matilda sleeping in the middle of the king-size bed. "We just got back from the lookout trail. Barney said you and Sophie went riding earlier."

"We're back now," I said, keeping my attention on my keyboard.

"What's going on?" he asked pleasantly, moving my way.

"I'm writing to William."

"Oh."

"I need to get back to work. I've been thinking about hiring a nanny."

Joe stilled, going silent.

"I think that might be easiest," I breezed on. "My hours aren't exactly regular, and I like the idea of Matilda getting used to one person."

"What?" Joe finally sputtered.

"For childcare," I said, proud of my matter-of-fact delivery as I looked up from the screen. This was harder than I'd imagined. "It would provide continuity. I mean, I don't have to be full-time right away. The Pettigrew House is close enough to the construction site that I can pop back and forth as much as I need. It's a great setup, really."

"We should talk about this," he said.

"What's to talk about? It's been the plan all along."

"I thought you were settled here."

"Why would you think that?"

"Because you seemed…"

"Happy?" I asked. I had been happy, and I could see now that was my big mistake.

"Yes."

"Well, I'm going to be happy in Windward now."

"Adeline, this is a decision for both of us."

"Wrong. It's my life."

His gaze flicked to Matilda. "She's my daughter, too."

I swallowed and hardened my heart. "You know the way to Windward."

"You're saying I should *visit*."

"Yes."

He drew back, and I hated the look of betrayal on his face. I wasn't betraying him. I was living up to our original bargain.

"I made these," I said, turning the screen toward him, hoping to shift the conversation. I'd felt empowered while I designed the business cards, like I was staking out my own turf. But now I had to force a hearty tone into my voice. "Professional or what? Graphic design software is amazing these days."

He looked at the card design. "What is happening?"

"What do you mean?" My chest felt hollow. Whatever

his culpability in plotting with my family, I knew I was blindsiding him with this.

"Did William ask you to come back?" Joe pulled out his phone.

"Don't you dare call William."

Joe looked up, clearly bewildered by my tone.

"This is my job, Joe. My life, my career, and I'm going back to it. Like we planned all along."

Matilda squirmed on the bed, vocalizing as she woke up.

Joe was quick on the draw and lifted her into his arms. He kissed the top of her head and settled her, still sleepy, against his shoulder. "You can't leave me, Adeline."

My heart hurt. For a moment, it actually hurt.

I cleared my thickening throat. "I'm not leaving you, Joe. I'm simply moving on to the next phase."

He did a double take at my choice of words, and for a split second I was afraid he knew I'd overheard.

"That was our deal," I quickly added.

"I don't like our deal. I want a new deal."

"You mean you want me to come around and do things your way? Their way?"

"I don't want—"

I waited, but he didn't finish the sentence. No surprise there, since me coming around was exactly what he wanted.

"I was never going to be Mrs. Governor Breckenridge. That was my dad's dream, Uncle Braxton's dream, your dream. My dream was to be independent and—"

"And free," he finished, sounding defeated.

"And free," I agreed, reminding myself how important self-determination was to me.

There was a hollow ring to his voice as he nodded at

the computer screen. "It looks like you're halfway out the door."

"You mean halfway to living my own life."

His jaw clenched and his eyes hardened. "Then don't let me stop you." He turned for the door, Matilda still in his arms.

"Joe!" I called out, irrationally terrified that he was taking her away from me.

He turned back.

I realized my fear was way off base. They were only going downstairs. I shook my head. "Nothing."

Comprehension seemed to dawn on him. He looked down at Matilda. "Can you imagine?" he asked softly, accusingly. "Can you even imagine not being with her?"

I couldn't. The door closed behind them, and I collapsed on the bed, my head whirling and my heart aching.

"Adeline?" Sophie knocked a few minutes later. After a moment, she opened the door.

I wanted to tell her to go away, that I wanted to be alone. But my throat was so tight, I couldn't make a sound.

She came to my side, sitting down, putting her hand on my shoulder. "I saw Joe downstairs. He looked—" A confused look slipped across her face. "What happened?"

"I can't do it," I said, my voice raw.

"What can't you do?"

"Stay."

She stilled.

"They never stopped plotting. They want me to be the good full-time political wife, by Joe's side through the election, and then move into the governor's mansion."

"That's a surprise?" Sophie squeezed my shoulder.

I pulled myself into a sitting position. "It shouldn't be, should it? How did I forget? Are they that good? Am I that gullible?"

"You're not gullible." She paused. "But they are that good. You've seemed so happy."

"I know." I nodded. "I am. I was. I obviously let my guard down."

"You're a new mom—sleep-deprived." Sophie gave a little laugh. "Survival is the best you can hope for those first few weeks. I know I'm still exhausted."

"You have Stone."

"And you have Joe."

I shook my head. "Not really. We're just pretending." I suddenly felt teary.

"Don't," Sophie said softly.

"It's hormones."

"You'll make me cry, too."

"I can't believe how hard it was to tell him." I vividly remembered the expression on his face. It was seared into my soul.

"What did you tell him?"

"That I was leaving."

"Oh." She sounded sad.

It was sinking into me now that I was truly leaving—Sophie, Joe, the mansion, everybody. And I was miserable about it. "How did my feelings get away from me like that?"

She took my hand in both of hers. "Adeline."

I closed my eyes, wishing I could go back to this morning—with the sun streaming in through my window, Matilda cooing in her crib, Joe's arms around me—when all seemed right with the world.

"You fell in love," Sophie whispered.

It took a moment for her soft words to register.

"With Joe," she added and tipped her shoulder against mine. "It hurts this much to leave him because you love him."

I shook my head in denial. I wouldn't have been that foolish.

They might have convinced me to marry him, but they couldn't convince me to love him. That one was up to me. It was all up to me. It was *only* up to me. And it wasn't what I wanted. Then or now.

My voice was a hoarse whisper. "I would never—" My throat closed and I couldn't finish. I couldn't voice the denial, because it was true.

Sophie cocked her head.

"Do you think he knows?" I asked with growing dread. If Joe knew I'd fallen for him, then he knew he held all the cards.

"He doesn't know."

"Don't tell him," I insisted.

"You have to tell him," she countered.

I pulled away, my voice a high-pitched squeak. "*Why* would I do *that*?"

"Adeline."

"Why?"

She shook her head. "In case he loves you back."

But Joe didn't love me back.

"I'm a political tool for him. That's not love."

"A political tool? You can't really believe that."

"You should have heard them, Sophie. Him and Xavier and Braxton. It was so…cold and calculated."

"He can love you and still want to be governor."

"It's way too convenient."

"Love isn't logical."

I couldn't bring myself to buy into her theory. "I'm his means to an end."

Sophie gazed at me a little longer. "Are you sure about that? You better be sure about that."

I nodded. I was sure, as sure as I could be, since the perfect Alaskan family was what Joe had planned all along.

Conversation felt stilted at dinner. I was uncomfortable, wondering who knew what, wondering if Joe had told my dad and uncle I was leaving, or if Sophie had told Stone I'd fallen for Joe. Kyle was away, and Mason left the table early to take a call.

Although Sophie did her best to keep up the chatter, I escaped right after Mason and pretended to check on the babies, who were with Marie during dinner.

"Adeline?" My dad followed me out of the dining room.

I stopped halfway through the great room, giving in to the inevitable, swearing to myself I'd hold my ground. I'd done it before, and I could do it again. The eighteen-year-old who'd insisted on turning my back on my home state and the family business and going to college in California was still inside me. And she was tough.

"Joe tells me you're going back to Windward."

I turned. "Of course he did." I'd bet the three of them shared all the gory details about me disrupting their plans. They'd already plotted their next move.

"Are you sure it's not too soon?" My dad's expression of concern might have moved me if I didn't know his real motive.

"The timing is perfect."

"Matilda is so young."

I didn't see any point in pretending any longer. "I've held up my end of the deal, and now I have a life to live."

"Don't do something impetuous."

"This is not impetuous. We did the engagement. We did the wedding. Joe got the chair appointment. And now we've had the baby. I'm tapping out, Dad."

"But there's so much more to—"

"You'll have to do it without me."

I saw Joe walk up before my dad did.

"Xavier," Joe said in a cautionary tone.

I was glad for the interruption, but I wished it wasn't Joe. I wished it was anybody but Joe.

"Adeline, if you'll just—"

"Leave it," Joe interrupted.

My dad turned on him. "You think you'll have better luck?"

"Got a minute?" Joe ignored my dad and spoke to me, nodding toward the patio doors.

"You won't have better luck," I told him with certainty, but I moved toward the door anyway. If the conversation had to be had, I was all for getting it over with.

We stepped into the sunny evening breeze. The days were longer and the sun was stronger as summer approached. I moved to the rail, watching the horses in the distance, focusing as they munched on the new green shoots, wishing my life was that simple.

Joe paused beside me. "You want to walk?" He gestured to the staircase that led down to the yard.

"Yes." I preferred to be out of my dad's and Braxton's view.

We took the long staircase to the backyard, then followed the concrete pathway that led to the edge of the woods, to the trailhead that went to the waterfall.

When I couldn't stand the silence anymore, I spoke up. "You told them."

"Not much."

Something rustled the bush beside us, and I took a reflexive step toward Joe as a rabbit hopped out of the underbrush and crossed the path in front of us.

He put an arm around my shoulders. "I'll keep you safe."

"I wasn't scared." I shrugged out of the embrace.

"Okay."

We walked a little farther on the packed dirt.

Joe broke the silence next. "So, this is what will make you happy?"

"You mean following my life's dream?" I asked, trying for sarcasm but not quite pulling it off.

He paused. "That's not a real answer."

"It is my life's dream." I was excited to go after it. At least I had been excited to go after it. Before my lovely Matilda came along, before my feelings for Joe got so complicated that I could barely work my way through them.

The sound of the waterfall came up in front of us, and we made our way out on the platform. A fine mist floated around us, cool and refreshing.

I braced my hands on the rail and stared at the rushing water.

Joe came up beside me, imitating my posture. "I want you to be happy, Adeline."

"Then we both want the same thing."

"But I don't want to lose you."

The mist dampened my face and my bare arms. "You'll know where I am. And I won't—" My heart hitched. "I won't keep Matilda from you. Not ever. I want you to see her as much as you want."

"I want to see her every day."

"You'll be in DC. You have your dream, too." Oddly, I wanted Joe to live his dream as much as I wanted to live mine. I wanted him to run for governor, and I wanted him to win.

"What if that won't work?" he asked. "What if me not being with Matilda, not being with you—with *you*— messes with my dream?"

"I can't," I said, and my voice cracked.

"No." He sounded contrite, and he shook his head. Then

he turned to me, looking contrite. He touched my shoulder, then he pulled me into his arms. "That's not what I mean."

I sniffed. I hated that I was tearing up. But I couldn't seem to stop.

"I don't mean for you to change," he continued. "I don't mean for you to give up everything. I mean for us…for me…for…" He drew a shuddering breath, and I felt the heat and the power and essence of him all the way through to my core.

"I love you, Adeline." His deep words seemed huge in the forest around us. His arms tightened their embrace. "I love you. I love you. I love you."

"Joe, I—"

He drew back, his palms framing my face. "Don't walk away. Give me a chance. Let me think of something. Let me find a way that we don't have to be apart."

"I love you," I said, gazing into the depths of his dark eyes.

A slow smile grew on his face. "Okay." He gave a nod. "Okay. So, there's that."

"There's that," I said, smiling back at him.

"It's a start." He wiped the mist from my cheeks, leaned in and kissed me gently on the lips. "Oh, Adeline."

"I love you." I said it again just because I wanted to.

He kissed me more deeply.

It was long minutes before he drew back for breath.

"I'll come with you," he said.

I shook my head. "Your campaign."

"You should work anywhere you want. Take on any project you want. I'll figure out how—"

"I can find something here in Anchorage." I suddenly, urgently wanted to meet him in the middle. "Or in Juneau." Urban planning happened everywhere.

"You don't need to—"

I put my finger across his lips. "I can juggle both." I was sure of it. "We'll take campy selfies and do media interviews."

"You'll help with campaigning?" He looked like he could hardly believe it.

"We both deserve our dreams." I knew we could do it. With a little bit of ingenuity, I knew we could have it all.

A broad grin grew on his face.

"You're thinking about Charmaine jumping for joy, aren't you?"

"I'm thinking about you." He framed my face with his palms. "How amazing you are. And how you are going to knock their socks off."

I felt myself mold against him. It was going to be the easiest thing ever to play Joe's adoring wife. My entire being sighed in joy and relief as he bent to me for another kiss.

Epilogue

The landscaping wasn't yet finished, and a few snow-flakes swirled in the crisp fall air, but the arts and cultural center was complete, and the community had come out in force to cheer the ribbon cutting.

The mayor's speech was over and the festivities had begun. We were inside now, out of the cold and enjoying the celebration. A local band was playing in the mezzanine, refreshments were being served in the big entrance hall and friends and neighbors were wandering through the complex, with tour guides stationed all around.

Little Matilda was behaving in Joe's arms, gazing around, drinking the world in like she always did. Next to a smiling Sophie, Lucas was squirming to get down, and Stone put his son's feet on the floor, holding his hands so he could pretend to walk. Lucas grinned from ear to ear with pride over his accomplishment.

Katie had flown up for the celebration, staying with

us in the mansion. She'd spent her summer in Alaska—
some of the time in Windward with me, but more of it
with Mason, who'd taken to flying down to Windward in
his Cessna at the drop of a hat to pick her up. I couldn't
tell where their relationship was going long term, but they
seemed very happy for the moment.

I caught sight of Nigel Long through the foliage of the
conservatory. I knew the governor was here, but this was
the first I'd seen of Nigel.

"Can you ignore him?" Joe asked me in an undertone.

"I'll try." I hated that Nigel had worked underhand-
edly against us, encouraged people to spy on us in our
own home.

"Let them play their little games," Joe said, his tone
completely unconcerned. "We'll beat them at the ballot
box."

"We will," I said with determination.

Joe's run for governor was going well. With two months
until the election, the polls showed him in the lead, and
he'd already picked up some notable endorsements. Governor Harland had been forced to play catch-up.

I saw Senator Scanlon arrive through the main door, her
appearance causing a little flurry of attention.

"I didn't know the senator was coming," I said.

"Neither did I," Joe answered.

"Want me to—" I reached for Matilda to free Joe up to
get to work. I'd learned from Charmaine and others that
you didn't skip any opportunity for networking.

"She's fine," Joe said, keeping hold of Matilda.

Nigel tapped the governor's shoulder and pointed to
Senator Scanlon. Governor Harland straightened his suit
jacket and immediately hustled her way.

I watched the byplay as Harland beamed a smile, putting out his hand to shake and glancing around, obviously

hoping the press would get a shot of the two of them together. Nigel took a photo with his phone.

"Coming up on social media," I whispered to Joe.

He grinned at me while Matilda smacked her little palms against his head, mussing his hair.

"Are you sure you don't want me to take her?" I asked again.

"Our vibe isn't DC uptight," Joe answered.

"It's messy father?"

"It's perfect Alaskan family."

To my surprise, Senator Scanlon only exchanged quick pleasantries with Harland and then moved on, her staff member—a young woman in her twenties—keeping up with her brisk pace.

The senator spotted Joe and angled toward us.

"Incoming," I whispered to him, at the ready to take Matilda.

"I see," he answered.

"Congressman Breckenridge," she said in a hearty voice as she approached, attracting the attention of the people close by.

Out of the corner of my eye, I saw my father spot her, assess the situation and head in our direction. You could always count on my dad to gravitate to power. Braxton was sure to be close on his heels.

"So nice to see you again, Senator," Joe said, shifting Matilda to one arm to shake hands.

"Hello, Adeline," the senator said to me.

"Hello, Senator Scanlon."

"Please, call me Rachel." She looked around the airy, bustling space. "I understand you're the driving force behind today's success."

"I was part of a team," I said.

"Don't let her be modest," Joe said, taking my hand. "She was at the helm the whole way through."

I saw Katie move in to take a couple of quick photos: Joe, me, Matilda and the senator. Charmaine had said Katie had a good eye for publicity shots, and I couldn't help but think Joe's trusty aide would be happy with these.

"Senator Scanlon." Xavier joined us.

"Xavier Cambridge. Hello, sir."

"I see you've met my granddaughter." Pride was clear in my dad's tone.

Rachel's smile went warmer still, and she reached for Matilda's hand, touching it lightly. "And aren't you the most adorable little girl."

Matilda grinned, then laid her head against Joe's chest.

"How's the campaign going?" Rachel asked Joe.

"Quite well—at least according to the polls."

"Brilliantly, according to the polls," my dad put in.

Rachel nodded to that. "I saw some of them. Debate prep?"

"Well underway," Joe answered.

"Good." She paused. "I'm looking at announcing an endorsement next week."

Joe's brow went up.

I didn't bother to ask this time. I reached out to gently lift Matilda from his arms.

Rachel winked at him. "I think you'll want to tune in for that."

"Thank you, Senator," Joe said, his tone sincere. "That means a lot to me, to us."

Rachel's gaze shifted to me and Matilda, then to Braxton, who'd just arrived. She smiled back at Joe. "You're truly the whole package."

I overheard Braxton whisper to my dad. "What?"

"Shhh," my dad whispered back.

Sophie and Stone moved our way.

Joe slipped an arm around me. "If by 'package' you mean the two best things that have ever happened to me. Then yes."

"You can tell that a mile away," she said. "Good luck in the election, Congressman. I know you'll be an asset for all of Alaska."

As she walked away, Joe squeezed me tight.

"That was—" I said.

"It was," he answered.

"Her endorsement?" Braxton asked on a note of amazement.

"I got some great pictures," Katie said, coming in close and showing them on her screen.

"Charmaine will be thrilled with this," I said to Joe.

"Hey," he whispered in my ear, drawing me a step back from the little crowd.

"What?" I looked up.

Matilda reached out and patted his nose.

"It's us," he said, gazing deeply into my eyes. "You, me and Matilda, over and above everything else. I love you two so much."

"I know." The private moment in the middle of the noisy flurry of people filled my heart. "We love you right back. So very much."

* * * * *

More great romances are available from
Barbara Dunlop and Harlequin Desire.
Visit www.Harlequin.com today!

WE HOPE YOU ENJOYED
THIS BOOK FROM

⬦ HARLEQUIN
DESIRE

*Luxury, scandal, desire—welcome to
the lives of the American elite.*

Be transported to the worlds of oil barons, family dynasties,
moguls and celebrities. Get ready for juicy plot twists,
delicious sensuality and intriguing scandal.

6 NEW BOOKS AVAILABLE EVERY MONTH!

HDHALO2021

COMING NEXT MONTH FROM

⊕ HARLEQUIN
DESIRE

#2863 WHAT HAPPENS ON VACATION...
Westmoreland Legacy: The Outlaws • by Brenda Jackson
Alaskan senator Jessup Outlaw needs an escape...and he finds just the
right one on his Napa Valley vacation: actress Paige Novak. What starts
as a fling soon gets serious, but a familiar face from Paige's past may
ruin everything...

#2864 THE RANCHER'S RECKONING
Texas Cattleman's Club: Fathers and Sons • by Joanne Rock
Pursuing the story of a lifetime, reporter Sierra Morgan reunites a lost
baby with his father, rancher Colt Black. He's claiming his heir but
needs Sierra's help as a live-in nanny. Will this temporary arrangement
withstand the sparks and secrets between them?

#2865 WRONG BROTHER, RIGHT KISS
Dynasties: DNA Dilemma • by Joss Wood
As his brother's ex-wife, Tinsley Ryder-White is off-limits to Cody Gallant.
Until one unexpected night of passion after a New Year's kiss leaves
them reeling...and keeping their distance until forced to work together.
Can they ignore the attraction that threatens their careers and hearts?

#2866 THE ONE FROM THE WEDDING
Destination Wedding • by Katherine Garbera
Jewelry designer Danni Eldridge didn't expect to see Leo Bisset at
this destination-wedding weekend. The CEO once undermined her
work; now she'll take him down a peg. But one hot night changes
everything—until they realize they're competing for the same lucrative
business contract.

#2867 PLAYING BY THE MARRIAGE RULES
by Fiona Brand
To secure his inheritance, oil heir Damon Wyatt needs to marry by
midnight. But when his convenient bride never arrives, he's forced to
cut a marriage deal with wedding planner Jenna Beaumont, his ex.
Will this fake marriage resurrect real attraction?

#2868 OUT OF THE FRIEND ZONE
LA Women • by Sheri WhiteFeather
Reconnecting at a high school reunion, screenwriter Bailey Mitchell
and tech giant Wade Butler can't believe how far they've come and
how much they've missed one another. Soon they begin a passionate
romance, one that might be derailed by a long-held secret...

**YOU CAN FIND MORE INFORMATION ON UPCOMING HARLEQUIN TITLES,
FREE EXCERPTS AND MORE AT HARLEQUIN.COM.**

HDCNM0222

SPECIAL EXCERPT FROM

⊕HARLEQUIN
DESIRE

*After the loss of his brother, rancher Nick Hartmann is
suddenly the guardian of his niece. Enter Rose Kelly—
the new tutor. Sparks fly, but with his ranch at stake and
the secrets she's keeping, there's a lot at risk for both...*

Read on for a sneak peek at
Montana Legacy
by Katie Frey.

The ranch was more than a birthright—it was the thing that
made him a Hartmann. His dad made him promise. Maybe
Nick couldn't voice why that promise was important to him.
Why he cared. His brothers shrugged the responsibility so
easily, but he was shackled by it. His legacy couldn't be
losing the thing that had made him. No. He couldn't fail at
this. Not even to be with her, the mermaid incarnate.

She smiled her odd half smile and splashed some water
at him again. "I don't think you even know all you want,
cowboy." She bit her lip, drawing his attention instantly to
the one thing he'd wanted since meeting her at the airport.
He followed her in a second lap of the pool, catching up to
her in the deep end.

"So your brother married your prom date?" She widened
her eyes as she issued her question.

"It was a long time ago." He cleared his throat. Maybe
Ben was right and he needed to open up a bit.

"Yes, you're practically ancient, aren't you?" She swatted
a bit of water in his direction, which he managed to sidestep.

"Careful, Oxford." He smiled, unable to help himself. It felt good to smile, even more so when faced with the crushing sadness he'd been shouldering for the past three weeks.

"Can you not call me that?" She paused. "My sister went to Oxford. And I don't want to think about her right now."

Her bottom lip jutted forward and quivered. It provoked a response he was unprepared for, and he sealed her concern with a kiss so thorough it rocked him.

Everything he wanted to say he said with the kiss. *I'm sorry. I want you. I'm hurting. Let's forget this.* Her body, hot against his, was a welcome heat to balance the chill of the pool. It was soft and deliciously curved. The perfect answer to his desperate question.

His tongue parried hers and she opened to him with an earnestness that rocked him. A soft mew of submission and he lifted her legs around his, arousal pressed plainly against her. She wrapped her legs around him, the thin skin of the bathing suit a poor barrier, and bit gently at his lip.

"I'm sorry," he started.

"Let's not be sorry, not now." Gone was the sorrow. Instead, she looked at him with a burning fire that he matched with his own.

Don't miss what happens next in
Montana Legacy
by Katie Frey.

Available April 2022 wherever
Harlequin Desire books and ebooks are sold.

Harlequin.com

Copyright © 2022 by Kaitlin Muddiman Frey

Get 4 FREE REWARDS!

We'll send you 2 FREE Books plus 2 FREE Mystery Gifts.

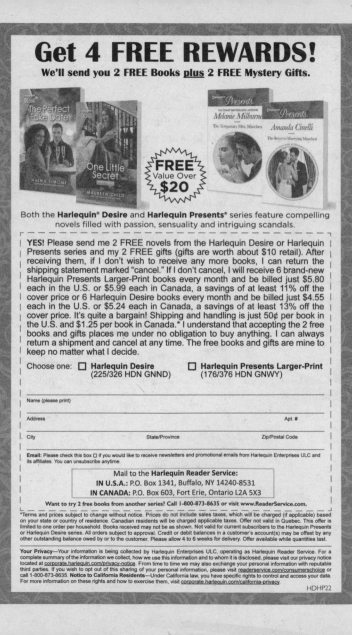

FREE
Value Over
$20

Both the **Harlequin® Desire** and **Harlequin Presents®** series feature compelling novels filled with passion, sensuality and intriguing scandals.

YES! Please send me 2 FREE novels from the Harlequin Desire or Harlequin Presents series and my 2 FREE gifts (gifts are worth about $10 retail). After receiving them, if I don't wish to receive any more books, I can return the shipping statement marked "cancel." If I don't cancel, I will receive 6 brand-new Harlequin Presents Larger-Print books every month and be billed just $5.80 each in the U.S. or $5.99 each in Canada, a savings of at least 11% off the cover price or 6 Harlequin Desire books every month and be billed just $4.55 each in the U.S. or $5.24 each in Canada, a savings of at least 13% off the cover price. It's quite a bargain! Shipping and handling is just 50¢ per book in the U.S. and $1.25 per book in Canada.* I understand that accepting the 2 free books and gifts places me under no obligation to buy anything. I can always return a shipment and cancel at any time. The free books and gifts are mine to keep no matter what I decide.

Choose one: ☐ **Harlequin Desire**   ☐ **Harlequin Presents Larger-Print**
                      (225/326 HDN GNND)   (176/376 HDN GNWY)

Name (please print)

Address   Apt. #

City   State/Province   Zip/Postal Code

Email: Please check this box ☐ if you would like to receive newsletters and promotional emails from Harlequin Enterprises ULC and its affiliates. You can unsubscribe anytime.

Mail to the **Harlequin Reader Service:**
IN U.S.A.: P.O. Box 1341, Buffalo, NY 14240-8531
IN CANADA: P.O. Box 603, Fort Erie, Ontario L2A 5X3

Want to try 2 free books from another series! Call 1-800-873-8635 or visit www.ReaderService.com.

*Terms and prices subject to change without notice. Prices do not include sales taxes, which will be charged (if applicable) based on your state or country of residence. Canadian residents will be charged applicable taxes. Offer not valid in Quebec. This offer is limited to one order per household. Books received may not be as shown. Not valid for current subscribers to the Harlequin Presents or Harlequin Desire series. All orders subject to approval. Credit or debit balances in a customer's account(s) may be offset by any other outstanding balance owed by or to the customer. Please allow 4 to 6 weeks for delivery. Offer available while quantities last.

Your Privacy—Your information is being collected by Harlequin Enterprises ULC, operating as Harlequin Reader Service. For a complete summary of the information we collect, how we use this information and to whom it is disclosed, please visit our privacy notice located at corporate.harlequin.com/privacy-notice. From time to time we may also exchange your personal information with reputable third parties. If you wish to opt out of this sharing of your personal information, please visit readerservice.com/consumerchoice or call 1-800-873-8635. **Notice to California Residents**—Under California law, you have specific rights to control and access your data. For more information on these rights and how to exercise them, visit corporate.harlequin.com/california-privacy.

HDHP22